National Best Selling Author

# K'WAN
### PRESENTS

A Novel By:

# SONNY F. BLACK

# GANGSTA
# BITCH

A Cold Hearted Hoe Is Tuff To Mend

D0674362

# GANGSTA
# *BITCH*

## SONNY F. BLACK

| LONDON BOROUGH OF HACKNEY LIBRARY SERVICES | | |
|---|---|---|
| LOCAT | No. VOLS | |
| ACC No. | | |

Life Changing Books in conjunction with Power Play Media
Published by Life Changing Books
P.O. Box 423 Brandywine, MD 20613

This novel is a work of fiction. Any references to real people,
events, establishments, or locales are intended only to give the fiction a sense of reality and authenticity. Other names, characters,
and incidents occurring in the work are either the product of the
author's imagination or are used fictitiously, as are those fictional-
ized events and incidents that involve real persons. Any character
that happens to share the name of a person who is an acquaintance
of the author, past or present, is purely coincidental and is in no
way intended to be an actual account involving that person.

Library of Congress Cataloging-in-Publication Data;

www.lifechangingbooks.net
13 Digit:  978-1934230367
10 Digit:  1-934230367

Copyright © 2011

All rights reserved, including the right to reproduce this book or
portions thereof in any form whatsoever.

# PROLOGUE

## 2003

**"Go ahead, you black cock sucker**. I want you to do something stupid, so I can toe-tag your ass."

D-Murder thought about it, but seeing the half dozen or so guns pointed at him he knew he'd never win. As carefully as he could he laid his pistol on the floor and got on his knees. Before he could even raise his hands the officers' dog piled on him, and they began punching him in various spots, trying to bend his arms at impossible angles.

Lying on his stomach, D-Murder looked around the room and wondered how the hell he had gotten caught in such a fucked up predicament. There was blood splattered on the overturned furniture and walls of the bedroom. A man he had never seen before lying on the bed with a quarter-sized hole above his right eye. On the floor beside the man was another body. This one was faced down with several holes in his back. Blood was still flowing from the body, turning the coke that had come from the busted packages into a pinkish goop. Though he had never once fired his gun, D knew he was fucked with a capital F.

"Somebody got caught with their hand in the cookie jar," an officer wearing a windbreaker smirked, cuffing D's hands roughly behind his back.

"Dawg, I know what it looks like but I ain't got nothing to do with this shit," D tried to tell the officer.

Windbreaker jerked him roughly to his feet. "Yeah, and I'm the fucking queen of England," he chuckled.

"Looks like that tip we got paid off, huh? Who we got here?" a black detective asked, approaching from behind. When he saw who Windbreaker had in custody all he could say was, "Oh shit!"

"What's the matter?" Windbreaker asked not really understanding the situation.

"That's D-Murder, from 128th."

Windbreaker turned D around and examined his bloody face. "You're shitting me. This can't be the so-called Ghost."

"It's him," the black detective confirmed. "I saw a picture of him at the house when we searched it."

"Wow, we've nabbed the fucking Boogie Man. Funny, I heard you were a lot bigger," Windbreaker examined him.

"Don't believe everything you hear," D-Murder said, as if he was being cleaver.

"You think this was some type of payback for what they did to his brother?" Windbreaker asked the black detective.

"Fuck is you talking about, what's my brother got to do with this?" D-Murder's smug attitude disappeared and was replaced by nervousness. "Somebody tell me what the hell is going on?"

"Probably," the black detective said to Windbreaker, ignoring D's question. "He was a big man when he was running shit, but now he's just meat. They tore that boy up something terrible."

Hearing them speak of his brother in the past tense caused D to panic. "What happened to my brother?" D tried to break loose. "Let me go, I need to find out what happened to my brother!"

"Calm down," Windbreaker ordered, putting D in a reverse chokehold. "Your brother ain't going anywhere but the morgue and your ass is going downtown, D-Murder."

"I told you I didn't have anything to do with this!" D continued to struggle.

"Right, those two stiffs shot each other. You're going down for double homicide, pal."

Windbreaker read D his rights, but he gave no indication if he heard or understood them. All that was on his mind was the pile of shit he had managed to step into. Even if he beat the murders they had still caught him with a pistol. He had been betrayed by his own crew and someone had assassinated his brother, the same man who he had promised his grandmother he would protect. There was no doubt in D-Murder's mind that even with a high-powered lawyer he would have to do some time. But no matter how long it took, D would have his revenge, this he swore on his brother's stolen life.

She stood watching the television in wide-eyed shock. The bowl she'd dropped along with the ice cream that had been in it, lay at her feet in a mess of glass and melting cookie dough. Even though the news reporter spoke with complete clarity, she still felt like she had heard wrong. This couldn't be happening.

It took a great amount of concentration for her to get her legs to move, but she was able to make it to the couch where she collapsed in a heap. With trembling hands she turned up the volume on her big screen television as the reporter recounted the breaking story.

"The bodies were found in this building," he motioned at the familiar structure behind him. Though she was never allowed inside, she had been to the building many times.

"Both men were killed in what appeared to be a revenge murder for the slaying of Dwayne 'Knowledge' Bernard, the boss of the Uptown Boys drug cartel, earlier today. The man in custody is one Derrick Bernard, alleged enforcer for the Uptown Boys and the brother of the deceased. The younger Bernard, armed with a loaded 9mm, was apprehended at the scene. Bernard is currently being held for the double revenge slaying as well as for questioning in several other murders that took place between 2000 and today. We'll have more news as the story unfolds."

She wanted to scream, but didn't have the strength to push the sound out, so the grief stricken roar she was looking for ended up being a sick meowing. She pounded her fists into the couch, trying to dismantle an imaginary opponent, until she was so spent that all she could do was collapse back on the couch. Pressing her tear streaked face into the cushions she prayed over and over for someone to wake her up from the horrible nightmare. When she opened her eyes nothing had changed.

*Okay, Francis, you gotta pull it together. We've prepared for this.* Pulling her self together as best she could, Francis tucked her emotions and slipped into Gangsta Bitch mode. The first thing she did was call the lawyer they'd kept on retainer for such emergencies. The second thing she did was pull out the safe she kept in the back of her closet. He'd always talked about putting it up for a rainy day, and from the looks of things, it was about to storm.

She counted the money twice and it still looked suspect. A double murder wouldn't be cheap and as good as the lawyer was, he was still a vulture. But this didn't deter her. For as feminine as she was, the heart of a hustler beat in her chest. As long as there was breath in her body and strength in her fingers, she would do any and all things in her power to protect her man. Grabbing her coat and a pair of leather gloves, she headed for the door. Before she left, she picked up her big black Coach bag and tested the weight. Nodding in approval she went out to make the rounds to try to ensure her man's freedom.

Though she meant well, it would only be a matter of time before the other shoe dropped, and when it did, it fell hard.

# ONE

## Five Years Later

**It was cold, but the sun was still shining**. Summer had rolled directly into winter, leaving everyone to wonder what in the hell had happened to the fall? The hood was quiet, but active. It was always like that in the winter. In the hood, some cats hustled like squirrels, stacking their paper through the warmer seasons and only periodically enduring the bite of the nastier ones. Then you had the goons, the young boys that are so hungry that neither weather nor warfare could deter them from getting a dollar. This was the case with Young Sha-Born.

"Big Pete, what da deal, baby?" Sha greeted his boss with a pound and a hug. He'd been on the block since five o'clock the previous day and showed no signs of slowing down.

"How we looking out here, son?" Pete asked. Pete was a young dude seeing good money slinging cocaine in the hood. Granted, he didn't have the deepest pockets or the largest crew, but he did very well for himself.

"Like money, baby, you know what it is wit this," Sha-Born clapped his hands together to try and warm them.

"True," Pete gave him a pound. "Yo, I'm going up-stairs for a few, son, anybody else ask tell em you ain't seen me."

"I see we into big things," Sha-Born looked at the girl Pete had with him up and down. She was the color of cinna-mon with long dark hair, and a shape straight off of Sticky Pages. Her sky blue jeans hugged her hips so crazy that Pete couldn't really be mad at Sha-Born for looking. Sha-Born wasn't sure where he'd found her, but he wondered if she had a sister.

"Always, kid, you know how the God play it," Pete said smugly. He pulled the sexy young girl closer to him. "But yo, you ain't seen me, my nigga."

"I got you, P," Sha-Born nodded. As Pete and the mys-tery lady passed, Sha-Born took one last look at her ass and sighed.

"These lil niggaz act like they ain't never seen a woman before," she said once they were in the lobby.

"Nah it ain't that, they just ain't used to seeing some-body as bad as you on the scene," he ran his hand down her arm. The elevator opened and they stepped in. Before the doors could close she was on him. The mystery lady shoved Pete roughly against the wall and jammed her tongue in his mouth. She stuffed her hand down his pants and began to massage his penis, while trying to suck the life out of him. By the time the elevator reached Pete's floor his breathing was ragged and he could hardly breathe.

"Give it to me, daddy. I want you to fuck me right here in the project hallway like a dirty little bitch," she panted in his ear while trying to undo his pants.

"Chill, ma," he broke her grip on his pants. "Let's go in the crib so I can bust that ass properly," Pete tried to sound cool, but his dick was so hard that he was starting to feel like he'd cum before he even got inside her. He undid the three locks on his apartment door and led her into his pad.

"Oh, this is fly," she looked around his living room in awe. There was a large flat screen mounted on the wall with a deep leather sectional opposite it. Lining his walls were beautiful prints of famous black leaders throughout history. The most impressive was a huge picture of Malcolm X greeting some of the locals during his tour of the Middle East.

"That was one bad mutha fucka," Pete said, motioning towards the picture.

"You're into Malcolm X?" she asked, seemingly impressed.

"Yeah, I've been following that cat since grade school. My father actually studied under him," Pete lied.

"Baby, you are *so* deep," she kissed him. "That's what attracted me to you. You're a street nigga, but I can tell you're really smart!"

"You gotta know things outside of the block. I be trying to school these little niggaz out here, but all they think about is paper and pussy."

"Speaking of pussy," she slid out of her jacket and undid her pants, "I've got something for you, baby."

"That's what I'm talking about," he ran his hand over her breasts through her tight shirt. He could feel her nipples hardening through her bra. "Damn, I need to taste these," he tried to lift her shirt, but she pulled away.

"In a second, daddy, I got something special for you," she raised his hand to her mouth and sucked his middle finger. She watched his eyes roll back in his head as she shoved it so far back in her throat that he could feel her tonsils. "Where's your bathroom?"

"Straight to the back," he nodded down the hall.

The mystery lady picked her shoulder bag up off the floor. "When I come back, I want your clothes off and your dick in your hand. I'm gonna fuck you so good that you'll think three times before picking a stray bitch up off the street," she promised before disappearing down the hall.

By the time the bathroom door clicked closed, Pete had yanked his sweater off and was working on his belt. He placed the small Glock he'd been carrying in his pocket on the coffee table and started working his way out of his pants. When he'd met her at the car wash on 149th the day before he knew he had to have her. Pete vowed that he would do any and everything in his power to sample the sweet fruit, but luckily he didn't have to do much. All he had to do was take her to eat on City Island and flash his bank roll and she was hooked. When he heard the door open, he sank back into his coolest pose on the couch, as naked as the day he was born.

"Are you ready to get fucked, daddy!" she called from the hallway.

"Ready than a mutha fucka," he replied, stroking himself to an erection. When she stepped back into the living room, his dick went as limp as a noodle.

"Surprise, you've just been fucked," the mystery lady smirked, pointing a very large handgun at Pete.

"Wh…what the fuck is this shit?" Pete stammered, looking at the pistol as if it was a UFO. The mystery girl's eyes had gone from star struck to murderous.

"A bake sale, mutha fucka, I want the pies and the cake!" she said with a hard edge to her voice that hadn't been there before. When she saw his eye twitch, she gripped the pistol a little tighter. "Don't get cute, son. Follow the rules and I ain't gotta lay you."

"Yo, I got a few grams in the freezer and some bread in my top drawer, but that's it. I don't shit where I live," he said in his most sincere tone. When her face softened he thought that he might've been able to talk his way out of the situation, but the gun slamming into the side of his face killed that thought.

"Son, I should lace ya fucking boots for even trying to insult my intelligence," she was leaning in with the gun pressed against his forehead. "Either get up and take me to the safe so we can get this over with painlessly, or I can pop you and find it myself, what you trying to do?"

"Listen, sister, I don't want no problems. You can get all of that," he slid off the couch with his hands raised above his head.

"Yeah, that's what I'm talking about," she backed up to let him pass, without allowing him to get close enough to try and grab the gun. "The faster you set it out, the faster I'm outta ya hair kid, this ain't the only stop I got to make today."

"Don't worry, ma, you can have that shit, it's nothing, but I hope you riding down on them white dealers like you doing us hood niggaz," he remarked.

"You talking shit?" she asked.

"Nah, baby, just trying to make a point. I mean, we all sling shit, but at least I'm trying to keep the money circulating through black hands in black hoods, what the fuck is the devil doing besides getting fat off our backs?"

She paused as if she was measuring Pete's words. He started to press his argument until the butt of the gun crashed into the side of his head. Pete dropped to one knee, and clutched his throbbing temple.

"Nigga, don't try to sway me with that fake F.O.I, shit," she jammed the gun into his eye roughly. "You talk about keeping the money in the hood like you're doing a good thing, miss me with that. You have black children selling your shit to other black people, so don't act like you're some fucking savior of our people. I'd be doing society a service if I finished you right here," her finger twitched on the trigger, but didn't squeeze. "Get your ass up and take me to the safe, pussy," she drew her hand back, but didn't strike him.

If it wasn't for the fact that he had a violent woman

standing behind him with a gun to his head, Pete would've kicked himself in the ass for getting caught out there so easily. Walking on shaky legs towards his bedroom, his mother's voice rang in his head. *Don't let the little head think for the big one.* Considering what was happening, he knew his mother was wagging her finger at him from the grave.

Shorty had a fly whip, was rocking jewels and was the baddest thing he'd seen in a minute. There was no way she could've been greasy, at least that's what he thought before he found himself being jacked. Opening his bedroom closet, where his safe was hidden, Pete made himself two promises; one was to murder the mystery woman if he ever saw her again and the other was never again to bring a female to his house.

"Drag that shit out here and pop it open," she ordered.

Pete reluctantly pulled the two foot safe from the closet and punched in the combination. The door popped open and as he tried to reach inside, he felt the cold metal pressed behind his ear.

"I'm about tired of you playing on my intelligence," she reached inside the safe and pulled out a berretta. She tested the weight of the gun before clubbing Pete in the eye with it. Blood gushed down the side of his face as he scrambled away from her. The mystery woman shook her head and tossed him a pillow. "Take the case off and fill it."

"Yo, you ain't gotta do it like this," Pete began slipping the case off the pillow, blinking the blood out of his eye.

"I know, but it's more fun this way. Now fill that case, yo," she motioned at the safe with her gun. Pete knelt, bleeding and cursing himself as he placed every dime he had in the pillow case. When the safe was empty he slid it over to her. She peeped in the bag and looked back at him.

"Nigga, they said you were balling," she laughed. The mystery lady looked at the expensive looking entertainment system. "Unhook that Blue-Ray and toss it in the case, and while you're at it you can set out whatever movies you got for it."

"Damn, shorty, you ain't gonna leave a nigga with nothing?" he pleaded.

"Mutha fucka you need to be thankful that I ain't taking your life," she reminded him.

Pete went about the task of unhooking his two day old Blue-Ray before going to the freezer and getting the work. When it was all said and done she could barely carry both of the pillow cases and her gun at the same time. She walked Pete into the living room and for a minute he thought his humiliation was at an end, but it was just starting.

"We almost done," she removed a roll of duct tape from her purse, "but I gotta tie up the loose ends," she proceeded to bind Pete's hands and feet. Once they were secure she used the remainder of the duct tape to tie him to the radiator.

"What you bout to do to me?" he asked fearfully as she approached him, digging around in her bag.

"Don't worry, big daddy, I ain't gonna hurt nothing else but your pride," she grinned wickedly, pulling her hand out of the bag, holding a small case.

Sha-Born couldn't believe his eyes. The sight was so crazy that he had to call his peoples little Dave and Mack, so they could vouch for the authenticity when he put the word on the streets. The three of them laughed so hard that tears ran down their eyes when they stumbled on Pete three hours later.

He was ass naked and tied to the radiator, but that wasn't the funny part. Before the mystery woman had left she had applied lipstick and eye shadow to Pete's face. He looked like a broken up drag queen, squirming around on the floor. The trio of young boys laughed at him for almost ten minutes before finally cutting him loose.

# TWO

**Arthur Kill Correctional Facility** was located deep in Staten Island, New York. It was a small compound, in contrast to other New York State prisons, but served the same purpose; to house and supposedly reform criminals. On the one hand, it was a blessing to be housed there because it spared family and friends the trouble of riding all the way upstate to visit their loved ones, but on the other hand… what the fuck could be blessed about a prison?

A guard sat behind the booth near the visitor's entrance/exit reading a Don Diva Magazine. She clicked her gum and thumbed through the pages, looking as if she could think of a million and one things she'd rather be doing than her job. At the sound of the automatic door that led to the bowels of the prison, she lifted her head and tried to seem alert.

Two guards came through escorting a young man who appeared to be in his early to mid-twenties. He had grown his hair while he was away, and now sported it in a messy pony tail, that showed his handsome face. His skin was ashy, but still smooth and youthful considering what he had just gone through. It had been five long years since the powers that be of the justice system informed him that he would more than likely be spending the rest of his natural life in a cage. Five years since he had felt the touch of a woman who didn't have an ulterior motive, the one woman he had ever loved other than his mother. Five years since the only family he had left in the world had been gunned down by some jealous niggaz for trying to feed his people. But at long last, he was free.

The female guard watched intently as the two escorts exchanged words with the young man before disappearing back through the automatic doors, leaving him alone. She waited until she was sure they were out of earshot before addressing the young man.

"Well, well, looks like somebody is going home," she said, beaming at him.

The young man returned her smile. "Thank God. After five years of fighting I've finally gotten my freedom back."

"I wish I could say I was sorry to see you go, Bernard," she addressed him by his government name. It was a rude statement to make to someone who was being released from prison, but there was no malice in her tone. She came from around the booth to stand in front of him. Reynolds was short with ass for days and big enough breasts to feed triplets. She didn't have the most attractive face, but what she lacked in looks she more than made up for in physique.

"Now, is that a nice thing to say to a man whose been wrongfully accused, Reynolds?" he asked playfully.

"You know I didn't mean it like that, but I'm gonna miss our little midnight shakedowns," she clarified.

For the last six months or so Derrick and Officer Reynolds had developed a *special* relationship. She was a bored housewife whose husband wasn't showing her enough affection. As with a lot of the female, and the occasional male, guards who worked the correctional system, she had sought comfort in one of the inmates she guarded. During the wee hours of the night, and sometimes morning, Reynolds would sneak him out of his cell and up to the laundry room. They would have fall down, drag out sex until neither of them could stand. There was no emotional attachment between them, so things worked beautifully. Reynolds got the gangster ass pounding that her husband was too stiff to perform and Derrick got to get some *real* pussy during his bid.

"Me too," he reminisced on their late night escapades. "But as with all good things, this too must come to an end."

"Not necessarily so," she removed a business card from her uniform pocket and placed it in his hand. "Give me a call when you get settled."

"I'll do that," he said, purposely brushing against her as he passed. He had almost made it to the door when she called after him.

"You know it still amazes me how you were able to pull this one off. A black man gets caught in a house with two bodies and five years later he's a free man? Who says the system doesn't work for us. One day you're gonna have to tell me how you were able to get that verdict overturned."

He paused, giving her his heart melting smile. "I'll think about it."

She could barely fight the urge to kiss those full lips one last time, but it would've been a fool's move with the cameras watching them. As mean as his cock game was, the departing inmate wasn't worth her job or her marriage. With a sigh, she watched him pass through the double doors and into freedom.

There was a small cluster of people standing outside the facility waiting for the bus. A woman clutched the hand of her unruly child as he screamed that he didn't want to leave his daddy. Derrick thanked his lucky stars that he didn't have children. There was no way he would've wanted his child to see him in prison. The moment his charges were rattled off and the iron door to his cell slammed shut he'd decided that any and all things associated with the outside world were as dead to him as he was to them. He even refused visits from those dearest to him. It was a hard pill to swallow, but it would've been even harder to do his bid with them on his mind. No, to suffer alone was better than to drag others into misery.

It would be a few minutes before the next bus to the Staten Island ferry came chugging along to pick up the passengers at the end of the line so the freed prisoner decided to do something constructive with his time. Pulling a piece of paper from the pocket of his faded jeans he dropped a quarter in the phone and punched in the number scribbled on it. By the fourth ring he was beginning to get discouraged, but on the fifth someone answered the phone.

"Yeah," the voice said, as if the caller was disturbing him.

"Inmate Brown, what it be like?"

"Young blood, is that you?" Brown's voice had lost its edge and was now pleasant.

"Yeah, man. I'm on the streets."

"Damn, they really overturned your shit?" Brown asked jovially.

"I got the paperwork to prove it, baby boy. Besides, you know the word of a snitch can't keep a stand up nigga down," the young man boasted.

"At least in your case, Duce," Brown joked. "How long you been on the streets?"

"About five minutes, but I'm ready to rock and roll." Duce assured him.

"You don't waste any time do you?"

"Dawg, they just stole five years of my life. I can't afford to waste time when I'm still playing catch up."

"I hear you, soldier. Tell you what, get yourself settled and give me a call. I got something lined up that you might be interested in, that's if you're ready to stomp with the big dawgz?"

"Nigga, you know my heart don't pump nothing but ice water. Once I get in the town I'll hit you back so we can set something up."

"Say no more," Brown said and hung up.

"One down," Duce said to no one in particular as he fished around in his pocket for another quarter. He dropped the coin into the slot and punched in another number on the payphone. This time the phone had barely rung twice before someone picked up.

"Yeah?" a voice answered.

"Cousin Reggie, what's good?" Duce said jovially.

"Who the fuck is this?" Reggie shot back.

"It's me, Duce."

"Oh, shit the notorious D-Murder," Reggie said.

"Come on cuzo that D-Murder shit is for niggaz that ain't fam, and that cat is laying in the cut until I call him out. You know I've always been Duce to you and auntie."

"Duce, I ain't heard from you in ages. How's life on the inside?"

"Shit, I wouldn't know. I'm on the streets."

"The streets? I thought they gave you like a hundred years?" Reggie asked suspiciously. Duce was his family, but he'd been there when they handed him the *long walk* at the sentencing.

"It's a long story, my nigga, but before you even run the risk of offending me with the question, let me give you the answer. I ain't snitched on nobody," Duce told him.

"Cousin, I didn't mean it like…"

"It's all good, Reg, but check it out, I need a favor

from you, son."

Reggie sucked his teeth. "Duce, I ain't spoke to you in five years and the first thing you crack on me for is a favor? Damn, just like a nigga fresh out the pen. Look, I ain't got no bread so…"

"Reggie, you should know better than anybody else that I ain't ever been strapped for no cash. I had more than enough bread tucked away before I got knocked and my paper game is still up. I need you to get me a pair of them knockoff Timbs in a size nine, can you do that for me?"

By 'Timbs', Duce meant *guns*.

"I don't know, D. You fresh out the joint so I know you're hot as a fire cracker," Reggie said.

"Cousin, you know I wouldn't ask if I didn't absolutely need it," Duce said.

"Everything alright, or do I gotta come down and see something for you, cuz?" Reggie asked seriously. He was known to be an asshole, but you could always count on Reggie to step up where family was concerned. They were about the same age and tended to get paired at family gatherings. When Duce and his brother got caught in the double cross, Reggie took it the hardest. Quiet as kept, he played a big part in the increase of bodies in Harlem in the months after Duce's arrest.

"Yes and no. Listen, it's a little hard to explain so I ain't even gonna try. All I'll say is that I'm putting my brother's affairs in order, smell me?"

The line momentarily went silent. Reggie had been a running partner of Duce's brother years ago so he knew the tragic tail without Duce having to rehash it. "A'ight, come uptown and see me tonight and I got what you need, yo."

"Bet," Duce said with a smile. "I'll come through the projects on the later side. Good looking, cuzo," Duce placed the receiver back on the cradle and exhaled. He had been a free man for less than ten minutes and he was already back up to his old tricks. A smart man would've fell back and tried to feel the world out, but not him. There were scores to be settled and the sooner he did, the sooner he could reclaim his life.

# THREE

**"Oh, now this one is hot!"** Mo declared, holding up a cream colored Chanel clutch bag that boasted a gold clamp.

"It's okay, but a little small for my taste," Frankie told her, while eyeing a slightly larger bag equipped with a detachable shoulder sling. "This is more my speed."

Mo placed the bag back on the rack and turned to Frankie. "Girl, you kill me with them big ass *grandma* bags. How you gonna step out in a mean dress with that big ass strap blowing the whole fit? A good clutch will always make a statement; you better get up on it, Frankie."

"Well, a tiny bag works for those of us who ain't got much to put in it," Frankie shot back.

"Yeah, I forgot you got a fetish for chrome, Frankie Five Fingers," Mo teased. She had acquired the nickname from her knack for making off with things that didn't belong to her. Ever since they were young girls Frankie had been a skilled thief, a skill that she sharpened in adulthood.

"Don't go there, bitch," Frankie warned her playfully. The two childhood friends went back and forth like that all the time. Frankie and Mo had been friends since the eighth grade. Even back then Frankie had a very low key style about her, dressing tomboyish but maintaining a natural sex appeal. Her mind spent more time on money than guys, but Mo was the opposite. She was a high-yellow girl with pretty hair who carried herself as if the world owed her a debt. The way men fawned over her and females hated on her gave Mo a sense of power which she exercised quite a bit. Back in school, Frankie would find herself fighting just about every Friday because of something Mo had gotten them into.

As they matured and their personalities surfaced, the two girls remained thick as thieves but their lives went in two different directions. While Mo went off to school, Frankie found herself knee deep in the game. There was something about the allure and dangers of the underworld that attracted Frankie like a moth to a flame. There was something about fast money that appealed to her more than the life of a square. Frankie couldn't see herself slaving at a job or being codependent on a man for her survival. Back then, her mind set was that nobody could do for her what she did for herself, but ironically enough it was a man who changed all that.

Their love for each other could've only been described as a blessing from God. Two tortured souls, seeking understanding in a world that had cast them aside as little more than statistics. She was the anvil and he the hammer that had formed an unbreakable bond, but foolish pride had done the seemingly impossible. For being his rider, his gangsta bitch, she was left holding the bag in one hand and a bleeding heart in the other. Frankie tried to forgive him and not curse his memory every day, but his mark was etched into her soul. The bitterness within her constantly fought with the love, but through it Frankie managed to keep her sanity, further showing that she was a stand up chick.

Frankie's cell phone ringing interrupted the girls' little debate over handbags, and her painful trip down memory lane. Placing her purse on one of the wooden benches, she began the task of retrieving her cell phone. Like most women Frankie kept a mess of things in her purse from lipstick to band aids, but unlike most women there was a nickel-plated .22 holstered in the zippered section of her bag that was reserved for wallets. By the fourth ring she had managed to snatch the phone from the bottom of the bag and answer it.

"Fuck took you so long to answer ya phone?" the caller barked.

"Well, hello to you too, big daddy," Frankie said sarcastically.

"Frankie, don't get cute. Where are you?"

"Me and Mo are on Madison Avenue."

"Y'all broads love to spend cake, especially when it's the next nigga's," the caller remarked.

"Boo, don't even come at me sideways. You know Frankie makes her own way," she said defensively.

"Damn, I'm only playing," he said, softening his tone. "Did you take care of that thing?"

"Yeah, old boy was looking like Rupaul when I breezed up outta there," Frankie went on to give him the short version of what had gone down with Pete.

"Damn that's some cold shit, Frankie!" Cowboy doubled over with laughter on the other end.

"Yeah, well I should've killed him and *your* ass for me having to kiss that rank breath mutha fucka."

"You gotta break a few eggs to make an omelet. But fuck all that, how much did you skin that nigga for?"

"Shorts," she snorted. "You said that mutha fucka was holding, Cowboy, but his lame ass only had about ten thousand in the safe. You couple that with the few ounces of coke and it was barely worth the trouble."

"Paper is paper, ma."

"Money isn't everything, Cowboy."

"Shit, I can't tell. You show me a broke nigga and I'll show you a potential suicide that just ain't happened yet. I can remember a time when ten stacks felt like a fortune."

"That was a long time ago," she replied.

"Wasn't that long ago, ma. When we first hooked up didn't neither one of us have much to call our own, but now we're getting it!"

"If you say so," Frankie said, thinking on the few hundred thousand she had stashed. It was a respectable nest egg, but hardly enough to pursue the kind of life she wanted. Cowboy was a product of his environment and as long as he had a few dollars coming in, he was content to stay in that environment, but Frankie saw the bigger picture. She knew there was life outside the hood and by hook or crook she was determined to make it.

"Say, before you come back uptown stop by One-Fish and snatch me some crab legs," Cowboy said.

"And who said I was coming back uptown?" she teased him.

"Where else would you be going? Girl, don't play wit me. You know I'd kill something over that."

"I know all too well," she said, thinking on some of his violent outbursts. "Anyway, we're gonna be down here for a while so I hope you're not starving?"

"Only for you, baby," he said as if he was the coolest cat in the world. "Oh, before I forget, there's been a change of plans for our date at that spot we were checking out."

"Here you go with this shit," she huffed.

"Why don't you shut your mouth and listen for a minute," he snapped. "Know-it-all ass female," he mumbled before continuing. "Yo, we're breaking Cos' man in on the caper."

"Hold on, you mentioned that Cos had somebody he wanted to put down but you never told me you were bringing him in so soon."

"That's because I'm running the show. You're the queen, but I'm the king of this court, ma," he reminded her.

"Anyhow, we're gonna pop the boy's cherry on the lick."

"Baby, I don't know about this. I mean, Cos is a true soldier, but that doesn't mean that his man is. There's too much paper involved to have some rookie nigga fuck it up."

"I hear you boo, but I trust Cos' word. He did time with son, and says he's official tissue."

Frankie huffed again. "I still don't like it."

"It ain't yo position to like it, Frankie," he said like a parent reprimanding a rebellious child. "Duke is gonna handle things with us on the inside and you bring up the rear, feel me?" Frankie didn't respond. "Woman, you hear me talking to you?"

She sucked her teeth. "Yeah, I hear you."

"A'ight then, I don't know what's up with you, but you better get it together before game time. Don't forget my crab legs when you come neither!" he said, before ending the call.

"Asshole," she said into the now silent phone.

"Who was that that's got you so uptight?" Mo asked, fumbling with the ankle strap of a pair of green stiletto heels she was thinking about buying.

"Dumb ass Cowboy," she grunted, tossing the phone back into her purse. "Sometimes that nigga gets on my last nerve."

"You sure know how to pick em, Frankie."

"Tell me about it. Sometimes he can be so sweet, but other times…I don't know, Mo. It seems like the majority of these niggaz ain't got a clue."

"Well, maybe you should bump your screening process up before you decide to get involved with these niggaz."

"Bitch, I know you ain't trying to pass judgment?" Frankie asked, with an edge to her voice.

Mo looked at her seriously. "You know me better than that. Look," Mo stood up, slightly unbalanced because she was wearing one stiletto and one flat, "you've been my bitch since back in the days. We've seen each other at our highest and lowest points and we know each other's personalities almost as well as our parents do. Baby girl, I can remember a time when you were on top of the world, because you had finally found someone to make you happy, but it's like a dark cloud has been hovering over you for the last few years."

"Mo, you bugging," Frankie tried to wave her off.

"Am I? Frankie, look at you. Girl you're gorgeous! It's nothing for you to bag a nigga that's got something going for himself, yet you keep hooking up with these low life little boys who ain't trying to see nothing outside of the block, all because your heart won't let go of something that you'll never have again. He's gone, baby. Frankie, I can't front like I know what it is to walk a mile in your shoes because you've been through some shit that has made the average chick break down, but bless your spirit, you always bounce back. Sweetie, heartache is a guarantee when you're from the bottom of the barrel, but the thing that I've found to be true is that there is life after love."

Frankie turned her face away, jaw tightening as she tried to retain some semblance of composure. "Mo, that's ancient history, so let's not dwell on it. I'm a new person, so old shit ain't got no place in my world, feel me?"

Mo just looked at her and shook her head. It pained her to see her friend in denial. "I hear what your mouth is saying, but the hurt in your eyes betrays your heart. Baby, you can tell yourself anything you want, but you can't lie to me."

Outwardly, Frankie scoffed as if Mo's words didn't move her, but they'd tapped a nerve. Her face was calm, but the look in her eyes was enough to make Mo swallow. There were few people who could've come at her neck like that and Mo was one of them. Mo had her flaws, but a lack of honesty wasn't one of them. She gave it to you exactly how she was feeling it.

The part of Frankie's brain that was still in denial wanted to tell her best friend that she was just hating because she didn't have a man, but Frankie felt the truth in her words. Frankie had a man, but she was still lonely and couldn't keep from wearing it on her sleeve. It had been longer than she cared to remember since she knew what it felt like to love, or even to be passionate about a man. She tried to convince herself that the flings she'd had in between love and familiarity had a snowball's chance in hell at capturing her heart, but it was a hard lie that Mo saw right through.

"Mo, I forgot I got something that I was supposed to do so I gotta get ready to shoot back uptown."

"I'll bet," Mo said in a disbelieving tone. "Do what you gotta do; I got a few more stops to make."

"A'ight, girl, so I'll give you a call later," Frankie said giving Mo a half-hearted hug and heading for the exit. She had almost made it out of the store when she heard Mo's voice.

"I still love you, Frankie Five-Fingers, even if you're still trying to figure out how to love yourself," Mo called after her.

Frankie's shoulders stiffened, but she didn't spare her friend a second look as she exited the store and stepped into the winter chill.

"Fucking females," Cowboy said, flipping the cell phone closed. When he did so the ashes that had formed on the tip of the blunt he was smoking dropped onto his white t-shirt. Cowboy ran his hand gently over the shirt, trying to dislodge the ash, but only succeeded in turning it into a stain.

"If you didn't have so many of them you might spare yourself some of the headache," the man sitting on the couch offered, counting out stacks of bills on the glass coffee table. He was in his mid-thirties with a slightly receding hairline.

"Man, to have just one bitch would be completely out of my character. A king has got to have a harem. You know how it is, daddy," Cowboy said, with a cocky smile. Next to Cos he was the elder statesmen and had the most experience in high-end crimes. Cowboy had been initiated into the game as a drug dealer, but it proved to be too much work and too many headaches. When that didn't pan out he turned to robbery and discovered that he had quite the knack for it. Cowboy quickly moved from stick up kid, to master thief, taking off bigger and better scores over time. Once he had the game down to a science he recruited a team and never looked back. They were a vicious group of young dogs who didn't see any score as being too big. Anything over ten thousand that got snatched in and around the hood, they probably had a hand in it.

"I hear you talking cat," the man said, placing the last of the bills on the table. "It's all there; you can count it if you want to be sure."

"We ain't gotta go through all that, man. I know you'd never try to beat me out of a dollar," he said, snatching the stacks of bills off the table and tossing them onto the couch beside him. Cowboy had been clocking the man's movements since he sat down with the money, but he would count it again anyway once he was gone.

"Alright, I've showed you mine, now show me yours," the man spread his hands as if his merchandise would appear out of thin air.

"I got you kid. Yo, go get that," Cowboy said to a girl who had been sitting quietly on the love seat. She was thin with skin the color of overripe bananas. She slid off the love seat lazily, flashing a touch of thigh from under her short skirt. The girl disappeared into the bedroom and came back out carrying a shopping bag. Without so much as glancing at either man she placed the bag on the coffee table.

"Check that out, kid," Cowboy nodded towards the bag.

The man laid the bag on its side and slid a shoe box out of it. After sparing a brief glance from Cowboy to the girl on the loveseat, he opened the box. Inside were an assortment of jewels of different shapes and colors. Even without his monocle the man could tell that the stones were of a high quality.

"That's what I'm talking about, son," the man said, running his fingers through the jewelry like the hair of a pretty girl. "This shit is even prettier the second time around, and worth every dime."

"It's actually worth a lot more, but y'all be hard on the God," Cowboy half teased him.

"Man, you know we gotta make our points too, Cowboy. It ain't easy getting rid of hot ass stones, especially quality shit."

"Nigga, you a fence. It's your job to get rid of hot shit so stop talking like you're doing me a favor," Cowboy said.

"Forever the ball buster," the man said, standing with the bag in his hand. "I'm outta here, kid. See you on the next go round."

"Fo sho," Cowboy patted him on the back as they walked to the door. "Yo, I might have some more shit for you in a week or so."

"That's what's up. You know I'm about a dollar," the man gave Cowboy dap. "See about me."

Cowboy closed the door behind the man and made sure it was secure. Placing the gun he had tucked in the small of his back on the table, Cowboy thumbed through the bills. After two counts it was still fifteen thousand, not bad for about 30 seconds of work. The two knuckleheads who had actually stolen the goods from a suburban couple's house in Long Island, only wanted five thousand for it. Cowboy, being no fool to the jewel game, gladly paid their asking price knowing that he would get three to four times more for it through his people. Just like that he had tripled his money.

"That's an awful thick knot you got there," the girl said slithering against Cowboy. She massaged his dick through the jeans. "Why don't you let me help you with that?" she breathed into his ear. The sensation made Cowboy shudder, but his face remained neutral.

"Damn, baby. You keep that up and it might be some shit in here," he told her.

"Come on, daddy, let me get that up out you," she stroked his dick a little more aggressively.

Cowboy thought about it, but came to his senses. "Shorty, you trying to get both of us killed. My girl is on her way and I don't need the drama. I'm bout to put you in a cab, ma."

The girl sucked her teeth and flopped on the couch. "Why I always gotta be the bitch to get put in a cab?" she asked, folding her arms.

"Because I say so, now get ya coat," he told her, flipping open his cell to call the cab.

"Cowboy you ain't shit," she said, snatching her jacket and storming towards the door.

"Bitch you knew that before you gave the pussy up. Don't let the door hit you in the ass on ya way out!" he called after her, doubled over with laughter.

# FOUR

**Duce got off the train** on 125th and St. Nicholas. No sooner than he cleared the stairwell exit he was assaulted by an icy blast to the face. Pulling the collar of his slightly snug bubble coat as high as he could without ripping it, he thought for the hundredth time how much he hated the winters, New York winters especially. Duce had spun the snow-covered yards of at least three state correctional facilities, but that was a different kind of cold, gentle even. New York City cold was different. Because of all the tall buildings acting as sort of wind tunnels it always seemed more brutal. Ignoring the cold as best he could, Duce headed west towards the projects.

Even with night falling and the frigid temperature people were milling about 125th street either shopping or plotting. The landscape was different than it was five years ago, but the vibe was still the same. Duce always thought of Harlem as being the epicenter of the entire city, if not the state. Each respective borough had its own flavor, but there was something about the allure of Harlem that most couldn't resist. In a sense, the heart of the city was focused within the boundaries of Harlem. Sitting off to the west was Duce's destination, the General Grant Houses.

Grant Projects brought back memories of Duce's childhood. When his family had first migrated from the south in the forties, this was where they settled. Though Duce's mother had moved them out sometime in the nineties it still felt like home to him. Over three generations of his line had rested and been bred in the projects.

His cousin Reggie lived in 430, which was the first building coming from east to west. His mother had moved to Georgia a few years prior, but Reggie remained. He had the finances to get out of the projects but refused to move. If you asked him why he stayed he would simply say, "This is all I know." Duce scanned the block for a payphone to call and let Reggie know he was in the area, but he didn't have to. He spotted his cousin standing in front of the building talking to two people.

The woman wasn't much to look at nor was she ugly. She was attractive in an "I'd hit it" sort of way. Her pink Phat Farm snorkel covered her upper body but from the curve of her thighs, trapped within skin-tight jeans, he could tell she was working with something. The man was about five-nine, maybe ten, with a freshly shaved head. Smoke rose in faint wisps from his dome, but he seemed oblivious to the cold. From the too-tight flight jacket and the man's pronounced movements Duce knew he hadn't been home long from a bid. He couldn't put into words how he knew, but he knew. While the woman was calm, the man seemed agitated and continuously moved his hands.

"Ray, why don't you relax," Duce heard the woman say as he walked up.

"I am relaxed, why the fuck you keep saying that?" Ray said, pacing slightly. "Yo, all I'm saying is that I wanna know what the fuck the deal between you and this nigga is?"

Reggie rolled his eyes off into space like he was tired of talking to the man. "Fam, ain't no deal, me and ya girl is just peoples," his voice was calm, but Duce noticed the fact that he kept his hands tucked into the pockets of his North

Face as he spoke.

"That ain't what the streets say. I'm up north for trying to keep a bitch fly and food on the table and niggaz is coming through telling me how she's fucking with some fat nigga from Grant," Ray declared, hostility in his voice.

From behind the thick glasses he wore Reggie's eyes narrowed to slits. Duce knew that deadly look from their childhood. Reggie had always been a little insecure about his weight. He had tried to shed it, but with little results. Reggie was a junk food junkie and the constant intake of sugar did little to help his weight problem. Still, commenting on it was a good way to get yourself into a scrap… at the very least.

"Yo, my dude, I'm trying to be humble about this, but you're gonna make me go there." Reggie said with the tension now clear in his voice.

"What?" Ray stepped closer. "You sound like you got some gangsta shit on ya mind, son."

"Come on, Ray, you're being a real asshole right now." The girl touched his arm only to have her hand smacked away.

"Fuck is you talking about? You act like you taking up for this nigga or something?" Ray glared at the girl, causing her to step back. "Word to mine," Ray turned back to Reggie, "I don't even like how you coming at me right now. Matter fact, take ya hands out ya pockets when you're talking to me," Ray insisted.

Reggie gave an exasperated sigh. "You don't want me to take my hands out of my pockets."

"Come on, Ray," the girl pleaded.

"Do what you do, money!" Ray had laid the gauntlet. Duce was about to step in, but Reggie's next move froze him.

Never taking his eyes off Ray, Reggie began drawing his hand out of his pocket. First there was the butt of the pistol, followed by the barrel. Reggie continued pulling and the barrel continued stretching. All three of the onlookers stood there in shock while Reggie pulled an impossibly long pistol from his pocket. The barrel was so long that the inside of Reggie's pocket had to have a hole in it to conceal the gun. Cool as a fall afternoon, Reggie pointed the gun at Ray.

"A'ight, my dude, this is the deal," he began calmly, "I fucked ya shorty a couple of times while you were away, but when you came home we both agreed that it was a wrap, end of story."

Ray just stood there stunned. He opened his mouth to say something, but no sound came out. He glared at Reggie so maliciously that if looks could kill he would've dropped dead, but a gun always trumped a look. This time when the girl touched his arm he allowed her to lead them away. Duce watched as they made their way down the path and across the street before he approached his cousin.

"You keep the block popping," Duce shook his head.

"You're one to talk, D-Murder." Reggie teased him. Duce laughed before leaning in to hug his cousin. "I missed you, nigga," Reggie whispered in his ear.

"Like wise, family," Duce told him.

Reggie held Duce at arm's length and looked him over. "You put on a little weight," he patted Duce playfully on the cheek.

"Yeah, it's amazing what confinement and a zero tolerance drug policy can do for your body," Duce smiled. "You should try it some time."

"Been there done that," Reggie waved him off. "D, I need to ask you something. Now, you know you're my first cousin and I would never come at you sideways, but I gotta ask. How the fuck did you get out of jail?"

"Ancient Chinese secret," Duce smiled at him. Seeing that his cousin was serious he went on to give him the details. By the time he was finished Reggie was just staring at him with his mouth open.

"You are one cold mutha fucka!" Reggie declared with an ear to ear grin. He knew that his cousin was ruthless, but had no idea how much so until that moment.

Duce just shrugged. "God has a plan for me. So, you got that thing I asked you for?"

"You get right to it, don't you?"

"I'm on borrowed time, cousin." Duce said seriously.

"A'ight, come on," Reggie led Duce into the lobby.

When they got into the elevator a woman wearing a fur that looked like a nappy carpet got on behind them. She was barley five feet and walked slightly hunched over. Her face was a picture of sagging jowls and a cigarette hanging between blackened lips that seemed to be locked in a permanent frown. Something about her struck a familiar cord in Duce but he couldn't place her. The elevator stopped on four and the woman shambled off.

"That dope is a mutha fucka," Reggie said, startling Duce a bit.

"Huh?"

"I'm talking about, Mary, nigga."

"That was Marv and Jamie's moms?" Duce asked in disbelief. He remembered Mary from back in the days as one of the parents who actually gave a shit about the kids in the neighborhood. She was a bright and jovial woman, but the fur clad thing that had gotten off on the fourth floor looked anything but. Just further evidence of how strong the call of drugs was.

Duce and Reggie got off on the seventh floor. Even if his cousin weren't leading, Duce would've know the way to the apartment. He had spent more than his fair share of summer afternoons with his cousins and aunt. Reggie unlocked the door and ushered Duce inside. The first thing Duce noticed was the smell of pine. The house was so clean that you could literally eat off the floor. Duce knew that his cousin was lazy as hell so he figured that he had a woman or two frequenting the apartment.

"Have a seat my dude, while I get the shit," Reggie motioned towards the living room. "You know where everything is so don't be shy," he patted the refrigerator and went into the bedroom. "You home nigga!" he called from down the hall.

Duce strolled into the living room with a familiarity that could have only come from spending a great deal of time in the house. The furniture and electronics were more modernized than Duce remembered it but in his mind it was still his Auntie Ruth's house. There was a picture on the wall with him and his brother Knowledge in their PAL uniforms. In the days before the money came into play everything was sweet, but that was a long time ago. Not wanting to travel any further down memory lane he settled on the couch and waited for his cousin.

By the time Reggie came out of the bedroom Duce was sitting on the couch watching television. He watched curiously as Reggie dragged what looked like a guitar case, only a square version, and placed it in the middle of the floor. Reggie fished the key from his pants pocket and undid the lock. Duce watched from over his shoulder and gasped when the case came open.

When Frankie entered the apartment she was immediately annoyed. The garbage can outside the kitchen entrance was overflowing and the house smelled like old chicken. Frankie knew exactly what the smell was because she had shared the meal with him three days prior. On the table sat three empty Heineken bottles that looked like they had been sitting there for God only knew how long.

Cowboy was lounging on the sofa shirtless, smoking a blunt. Though his chest and arms were still quite muscular, his belly protruded over his jeans a bit. Just another sign that time was catching up with him. Cowboy was almost ten years older than Frankie, but still carried himself with the immaturity of a man fresh into his twenties.

"I see you've been busy," Frankie said sarcastically. She dropped the bag with his crab legs on the coffee table hard enough to rattle the bottles.

"Yeah, been a long day," he replied, in an equally sarcastic tone. "Thanks," he nodded at the bag of food.

"Whatever," Frankie mumbled, storming off into the bedroom. She had expected to find an equally disturbing mess there too, but it was surprisingly spotless. The sheets had been changed and the carpet was freshly vacuumed. It was too unlike Cowboy, so her antennas immediately went up. Frankie combed every inch of the room and all her search yielded was a pair of dingy blue, Polo boxers under the bed.

"You're bugging out, Frankie," she said to herself. Frankie felt like a fool for crawling around on her hands and knees like a damn forensic scientist. Thankful that no one had been there to witness the spectacle, she got off her knees and made to take the boxers to the laundry hamper, which was also overflowing. She'd knock the laundry out for him later, but first she needed to get right. It had been a few days since Cowboy had bust her out and she had a new lingerie set she wanted to show off. The smile faded from Frankie's face when she smelled the faint scent coming from the boxers.

Frankie held the boxers as close to her nose as she dared and her face twisted. The smell was soft like honey, with faint traces of musk lurking beneath. When she examined the underpants and saw the dried smear near the cockhole her hands began to tremble with rage. "Dirty son of a bitch," she snarled. With the boxers clutched in her fist she made her way into the living room to confront Cowboy.

The moment he saw Frankie's face, Cowboy detected that something was wrong. Though she was smiling pleasantly there was tightness to her eyes that made him uncomfortable. When his Polo boxers came sailing across the room and landed on his lap he knew he had a problem.

"You think you're slick, don't you?" she snapped. Her fists were balled so tight that you could hear her knuckles cracking.

"Girl, what the hell are you talking about?" he asked as if he was really clueless.

"Cowboy, don't play with me. Why do your boxers smell like another bitch?"

"Frankie, you tripping, I've been in the house all day."

"Yeah, with another bitch," she jabbed her finger at him.

"Man, don't come at me with that shit. You know don't no bitch come up in this pad but you."

Out of nowhere Frankie slapped Cowboy's food off the table, splattering him with the warm butter he had been dipping his crab legs in. "Nigga, don't you dare insult my intelligence!"

In a flash, Cowboy was on his feet and advancing towards Frankie. "Bitch, you must've lost your damn mind. I ought to knock your fucking head off!"

Equally fast Frankie grabbed her purse and dipped her hand inside. "I wish the fuck you would act a fool in here, Cowboy."

Knowing what she had inside the purse Cowboy stopped in his tracks. "Frankie, if you draw that gun on me you better pop off."

"Baby, you know Frankie Five-Fingers don't bluff," she said in a sweet tone. "Let me explain something to you,

Cowboy, I'm not a dummy. I know you do your thing on the side, but I turn a blind eye to it because you've always let it be known that I was the queen bitch and treated me with respect, until now."

"Baby it ain't what you think."

"Fuck what I think, it's what I know." She sucked her teeth. "I don't even know why I fuck with your sorry ass. You ain't shit, Cowboy," Frankie slung her purse over her shoulder and headed towards the door.

"Baby girl, don't walk away from me now, I need you for the score tonight!" he called after her.

"Fuck you!" she shouted before slamming the door.

"Damn it!" Cowboy slammed his fist on the coffee table, almost breaking it. He knew that without evidence Frankie couldn't convict him, but her storming out wasn't what had him uptight. He had a sweet lick lined up that the two of them were supposed to take off that night and now he found himself a man short. Though his crew consisted of four seasoned thieves, he chose to take Frankie because he wouldn't have to give her an equal split of the take. She was his girl so what was hers was his, and what was his was his.

"Fuck it. Time to go with plan B," he said, flipping open his cell phone.

The entire case that Reggie had dragged into the living room was filled with guns. As far as guns went he had everything from American Colts to German Rugers. Duce picked up a black 9mm and tested the weight in his hands.

"That there is new," Reggie nodded at the gun, while snacking on a doughnut. "That little piece of iron can lay low the mightiest of men, cuzo. Be careful because there's one in the head already."

"I like this shit," Duce said, practicing his aim. "I can do a nigga dirty with this."

"Yeah, that shit has stopping power, but I like the more messy shit," Reggie reached under the couch Duce was sitting on and pulled out a rifle. It had a long sleek barrel and a large scope on top. "See, you can blow a nigga's whole chest cavity out and never have to get up on him. You can survive a shot from a nine, but ain't no coming back from a .33."

"You can keep that shit, Reggie; I wanna get up close on this one. I need a nigga to feel my pain," Duce said emotionally.

"So, you about to make that right, huh?" Reggie asked. His normally jovial tone had become serious.

Duce looked at him with sad eyes. "If I can. Reggie, the five years I was in prison I never got one peaceful night's sleep knowing that these niggaz was out here enjoying life and my brother was in the ground. In a sense, I felt like a coward for not doing anything about it. I gotta settle this debt, cousin."

"You know I got ya back, right?" Reggie balanced on the rifle.

Duce looked up at him. He didn't say what he was feeling because he was sure his cousin already knew. "Cousin, if I need you then I'm sure as hell gonna take you up on it, but for right now I'm going in alone."

"Well, the offer is open. Just say the word and it's on," Reggie said.

Duce smiled. It was good to know that there were a few *real niggaz* left. "Thanks, family, I'll come see you soon and let you know what's up." Duce picked up a Glock, which was slightly smaller than the 9mm he'd selected. "I'm gonna take these off ya hands and get up outta here."

"You bout to put in that work?" Reggie asked excitedly.

Duce chuckled. "Not yet, Rambo, it's just somebody I want to check up on. When the sun goes down, that's when niggaz will start bleeding." He slipped the 9mm into his coat pocket and the Glock into his jeans.

"So be it," Reggie nodded. He picked up three clips from the case and handed them to his cousin. "Never can be too careful," he said leading him out the door.

The two men waited for the elevator in silence. Duce could tell by the look on Reggie's face that he wanted to say something, but the men in their family were never good at putting their feelings into words. Instead of talking, Reggie just tapped the elevator button. When the small box car opened, Duce gave his cousin another hug and stepped in. The doors started to close, but Reggie's chubby hand stopped it.

"You know how to reach me if you need me, so don't hesitate," he said seriously.

"I won't," Duce said as the door slammed shut.

# FIVE

**The tears didn't come** until Frankie was inside the cab and away from Cowboy's apartment. As strong as she was she always seemed to play the fool for Cowboy. Just like with most men, he was the perfect gentleman when they were dating, but also like most men, he started showing his ass once she had committed to him. Mo had asked her time and again why she continued to deal with Cowboy's womanizing ass and she always had a good excuse, but the truth of the matter was that she was lonely.

Frankie had been getting money here and there on her own, but since Cowboy come along she wanted for nothing, but it wasn't the money that kept her with him. Cowboy represented a piece that Frankie had lost a long time ago. His soul might not have been a perfect fit, but it mended the hole well enough. Sometimes it was just being in his arms that made her feel whole, but it was a temporary relief. There was only one man in her life that had ever made her feel like a *real* woman and he was gone, never to return. She thought about her lover often, the good times, the late night talks, but with the good came the bad. The man she had once given her heart to left her for dead and that was a scar that would never heal.

Frankie had been so lost in her thoughts that she hadn't

even noticed the cab had stopped. She paid the man and climbed out. When her foot touched the icy curb, she almost lost her balance. "I hate the fucking winter time," she mumbled, pulling herself the rest of the way out. Moving as gracefully as a cat burglar, she managed to make it to her building without busting her ass. While Frankie was fishing around for her keys, the hairs on the back of her neck stood up. She fingered her gun and using the reflection off the building's entrance she scanned the area behind her. She missed him on the first sweep, but on the second her eyes caught him. He was standing on the other side of the street, watching Frankie. She couldn't see his face, but the way he held himself was familiar. When it hit her, Frankie's breath caught and she whirled around. A bus rolled down the avenue, momentarily obstructing her view, and when it moved the sidewalk was empty.

It took her several tries, but Frankie was able to insert her key and let herself in the building. Her breaths came in short bursts as she stumbled into the lobby and closed the door. She stood there for a minute, back pressed against the heavy door, and tried to get her thoughts together. "I'm bugging the fuck out," she told herself. She reached into her bra and pulled out the fifty of haze she'd bought on the way home and threw it on the ground. She reasoned that once you started seeing ghosts it was time to stop getting high.

Duce pressed himself against the drawn gate of the recently condemned bodega. The gate's frozen metal touched his back, even through his coat, but he welcomed it. He needed something to focus on besides his racing heart. From the way her body went rigid he was sure she'd spotted him. Thankfully the bus and its untimely arrival had kept her from making a positive ID. Exposing his hand too early would complicate things, and this was a plan he needed to go off without a hitch. He had told himself that it was a bad idea, but he had to come, he needed to *see* her.

He cursed himself for being so careless, but sometimes the heart makes lumbering oxen of the graceful men. Every ounce of him wanted to swoop in on her, to let her look into his face and gasp, but it would have to wait. There were people he needed to see before he could go to Frankie. When his business was finished he would lay his heart open to her and if she stuck a knife in it, he could only fault himself. Sparing one last glance at Frankie's back as she slipped into the building, Duce went off to handle his business.

The livery cab wove in and out of traffic like a mad man. Several times Duce had to tell him to slow down. The last thing he needed was for them to get stopped while he was carrying two hammers. He hated taking cabs, but hadn't had a chance to pick his truck up yet. A friend of his had been housing it in his garage out in Long Island. Duce made a note to himself to call his man and make arrangements for the truck to be dropped off.

Duce pulled a Newport from his pack and tapped it against the back of his hand. Five years ago he frowned on smokers, but after what he had been through he understood the habit a little better. No sooner than he lit it the cab driver started beefing. A cold glare and the promise of a ten dollar tip quieted his grumbling. Reclining back in the seat he tried as best he could to get his thoughts together. Just seeing Frankie brought back old feelings that he needed to be buried for him to function properly. "Business first," he reminded himself. When he was within three blocks of his destination he had the driver let him out on the corner.

Just being back on the East Side brought back memories. He and his brother had run all up and down Second Avenue, chasing girls and getting money. When they had first set up shop in Wagner projects they met heavy opposition. It seemed like just about every other day Duce was shooting at somebody or somebody was shooting at him. The bullshit calmed down when Knowledge gave the young boys from the neighborhood positions in the organization. Had Duce had it his way, he would've just tried to kill everyone that came at them, but that wasn't how Knowledge did things. "Diplomacy over bloodshed, little brother," he would always stress to him.

Duce pulled his skull cap low over his ear and entered the projects. The cold weather had caused most of the residents to seek shelter in the warmth of their apartments; business still had to be conducted. To the untrained eye the young men wondering in and out of the various buildings and cuts would've seemed little more than residents coming and going but Duce knew better. For as long as he could remember Wagner had been a gold mine.

Though Duce had been a phantom in his days as D-Murder, there was still a chance that someone might recognize him and compromise his plan. He needed a way to locate his enemies without being detected too early, and the crack head shuffling past him would do nicely.

Though he couldn't remember her name, he knew who she was. She had lost about 40 pounds since he'd last seen her but for the most part her features were the same. The woman in question was as thin as a rail and sporting a short afro that looked like it hadn't been combed in days. Back when Duce and his brother ran through the projects she was lacing her blunts with cocaine, but now she was just a base head. Smoker or not, a base head was still the best source for information in any hood.

"Yo, ma, let me holla at you for a minute," Duce called

after her. She stopped and glared at him suspiciously, but did-n't come any closer.

"Fuck is you the police?" she snaked her thin neck.

Duce laughed as she was still as feisty as ever. "Nah, I ain't no roller, sis. I used to pump around here with Knowl-edge. I'm fresh home from a bid and trying to get a pack. You don't remember me?" Duce asked, hoping she didn't.

The crack head took a few steps towards him, squint-ing. "Can't say that I do, but if you looking for Knowledge then you might wanna try Rose Hill Cemetery. Somebody blew his brains out a few years back."

"Damn, I didn't know that," Duce lied. "Who I gotta see to get right?"

"Do I look like the damn information clerk at Macy's? My time is precious, sweetie," she said, scratching her neck and looking around nervously. It was obvious her monkey was clawing its way up her back.

Knowing what time it was, Duce pulled a $20 from his pocket and dangled it in front of her. "Ain't no need for the attitude, ma, I'm out here chasing a dollar like everybody else."

"I'll bet," she said, snatching the bill and stuffing it into her dingy bra. "Since you've been gone I know you prob-ably ain't up on it, but Butch is running the show now."

Duce's jaw tightened. Back in the days Butch had been a part of their crew. The seasoned hustler had been fresh home from prison and Knowledge didn't hesitate to put him in position. The old head was one of Knowledge's most trusted lieutenants back then. He was the left hand while Duce was the right. He had sent Duce letters from time to time while he was away, but six months into his bid the letters stopped coming. The next thing you knew Duce was hearing stories about how Butch was the nigga to see on the East Side, and how he was bragging about taking what Knowledge once held. Duce was never sure exactly what Butch's role in Knowledge's murder had been, but he would catch it like the rest of them.

"Sis, I got another dub for you if you can point me to him," Duce offered.

The crack head looked at Duce as if he had insulted her. "Baby, 40 funky ass dollars couldn't get you that type of information, even if I did know where he was. Butch don't come around here much. He does all his business through Scott these days."

Just hearing Scott's name made Duce want to go ballistic. Scott was a soldier in his brother's organization. Duce remembered him as a loud mouth little bastard that was in a rush to die. On the day he took his fall, it was Scott who had placed the phone call telling him that the spot was being robbed.

"Little Scott still running round out here?" Duce asked in an easy tone.

"He ain't little no more. Since Butch took over, Scott's been running around here like he was Ivan the Terrible. It's a miracle ain't nobody killed or locked his ass up yet," she told him.

"Man, I ain't seen my nigga Scott in years, he around now?"

"Nah, I ain't seen the little fucker in a few days. He'll probably be poking his head out sooner or later to come see his baby mama Marsha."

At that statement Duce felt like all the wind had been sucked out of him. At the time of Knowledge's death, Marsha had been his shorty. The more the crack head spoke the thicker the plot got.

"Damn, Marsha still lives in the projects?" he asked almost innocently.

"Sure do. You'd think with all the shit her man sling

he'd have moved her out, but the bitch is still up on the eleventh floor. She came through here not too long ago, swinging that fake ass weave."

Duce handed the crack head two more twenties. "Good looking out, ma."

"For what, I ain't did shit?" she asked, confused.

"Love, you did more than you know," he said, before leaving her standing there in a state of confusion.

# SIX

**"Yo, I wanna thank you for** finally trusting me enough to get some money wit you, Poppy. I was trying to get wit you for a minute, yo," Rico said excitedly.

"No doubt," Cowboy mumbled, never taking his eyes off the front of the bodega. He thumbed the handle of his gat and found it came away moist with sweat. He was nervous, but wouldn't allow Rico to see it.

"For real, yo, you've been like my idol since back in the days. Yo, you like the black Jesse James, B. Word to my dead moms I cant wait to go up in there and take these Spanish niggas' shit!" he continued to babble.

The more Rico talked the more annoyed Cowboy seemed to become. Frankie backing out at the last minute had almost led to Cowboy aborting the mission, but once he had his mind set to do something, nothing short of death or paralysis could deter him. He could've called on Cos or Thor, but they would've more than likely tried to talk him out of the foolish caper. El Pogo was a beast and was known throughout the underworld for his connections and brutality. To rob him was just as good as slitting your own throat, unless you were lucky enough to get away with it, which Cowboy felt he was. For as cunning and ruthless as Cowboy was, he knew he couldn't pull the caper off alone. He needed someone to watch his back while he cleaned the place out; this is where Rico came in.

Rico was a young knucklehead from the neighborhood who was determined to make a name for himself in the game. Though Rico wasn't the most seasoned criminal, he would follow directions and kill on command. He had been hounding Cowboy to put him in position for the longest, but Cowboy kept a close circle and was hesitant to let outsiders in, especially those who weren't proven or didn't come with a damn good reference. Frankie's bullshit move had backed him into a corner and forced his hand, which was the only reason Rico was sitting in the passenger seat of the mini van.

Finally, having enough of the young man's constant chatter, Cowboy addressed him. "Rico shut up and listen. These ain't no fucking chumps we about to ride on, so calm the tough talk. You fuck up and El Pogo will make a necklace outta your balls, make no mistake about that. All you gotta do is follow my lead and let's get this money." Without waiting for a response Cowboy got out of the van and headed towards the bodega.

The little bell over the front door of the bodega was drowned out by the sounds of Latin music coming from the wall mounted speakers. Cowboy headed towards the counter while Rico went behind the shelf towards the beers. "Hurry up, my dude, them hos ain't gonna wait forever," Cowboy shouted to Rico.

A Hispanic woman who looked to be about in her forties manned the register while a slightly younger man made sandwiches. The woman gave Cowboy the once over as he approached.

"Mommy," he addressed the woman behind the register, "let me get a pack of Newports and two Dutch Masters," Cowboy said, digging in his coat pocket like he was looking for his money.

"Regular or one hundreds?" she asked, reaching above the counter to the cigarette rack.

"Both bitch!" Cowboy said, pulling a nine out of his coat pocket and shoving it in her face.

"Take it easy, Poppy, I give you the money," the woman said nervously.

"Fuck what you got in the drawer, I want the *real* money. And while you're at it, set out that yay." Cowboy said. When the woman didn't move, Cowboy did. Using his free hand, he grabbed her by the front of her floral blouse and pulled her roughly over to his side of the counter. "Don't make me push your shit back, ma. Just set the coke and the dough out and I'm on my way."

"Get the yay, ho, you know what it is!" Rico screamed at the woman, but kept his gun trained on the young man behind the deli counter.

"You mutha fuckas know who you're robbing?" the delicatessen worker seethed.

"Don't I look like I know who I'm robbing?" Cowboy directed his gun in his direction.

"Fuck you and El Pogo!" Rico said excitedly. From the way he was bouncing in place, Cowboy hoped he didn't shoot anyone by accident.

"Tell me how we gonna do this, bitch," Cowboy yanked the woman roughly to her feet. If it weren't for the fact that he was holding her upright her knees would've probably given out from fear. "We're gonna go in the back and get the coke. You play nice, you live, you fuck with me and I'm gonna fuck your old ass before I body you, comprende?" The woman was hesitant at first but seeing that Cowboy meant business, she complied.

With Cowboy's gun pressed firmly to the back of her head she led him through a pair of double doors and through the store room to the back office. Through the small glass window of the door Cowboy could see two men sitting around a table packaging drugs. Keeping the woman in front of him like a shield, he shoved the doors opened. One of the men was instantly on his feet, but froze when he saw the black man holding a gun to the woman.

"Don't get up on my account," Cowboy said to the men, making sure to keep the woman's body between the men and him. One of them eyed the Glock sitting on the table like he wanted to play hero so Cowboy gave him some food for thought. "I want you to, so I can peel this bitch and still drop you before you draw." This gave the man pause. Cowboy pulled a heavy duty trash bag from his waistline and tossed it onto the table. "Shovel all that powder and whatever dough you got in the bag. If I don't feel like you're moving fast enough, this old bitch is getting it!"

"I ain't giving you shit. El Pogo is gonna smoke your black ass," a man sporting a handlebar mustache said smugly.

"Oh, you must think I'm playing, huh? Well, let me see if I can show you just how serious I am." The sound of thunder filled the store room, followed by the man with the mustache's bicep exploding. He shrieked like a wounded animal before collapsing to the floor, clutching his wounded arm. "Now, the next nigga come at me with some tough guy shit is taking a fucking nap, we clear on that shit?"

"Please don't kill me," the woman sobbed.

"Baby, I ain't trying to kill nobody, just do like I tell you to and everything is gonna be okay," Cowboy dug into his pocket and pulled out several plastic restraints. "Get over there and tie your amigos up." Not wanting to be the next one to catch a bullet the woman did as she was told. While the woman was tying the men up, Cowboy started tossing money and cocaine into the garbage bag.

"You're not gonna get away with taking El Pogo's shit!" the wounded man with the mustache hissed.

Cowboy flashed a smug grin. "In case you hadn't noticed, I already have." Ignoring the larcenous glares that were coming his way, Cowboy continued to stuff the bounty into the bag. He couldn't help but to smile thinking about what he was going to charge Butch for the cocaine. El Pogo's shit would draw top dollar. "Another smooth lick," he mused to himself, but that quickly turned into a feeling of dread when he heard the gunshots coming from the front of the store.

The sound of gunfire coming from the store room distracted Rico long enough for the deli worker to make a move. In a swift motioned he grabbed a .25 that had been stashed in the bread container. God must've been with Rico because just before he would've gotten his head blown off; a young man walked into the store, jingling the bell over the front door. Rico turned his head just in time for a bullet to nick his cheek and puncture a can of peas on the shelf behind him. More out of fear than anything else, Rico started letting off with the Colt.

Glass and food flew inward as the powerful slugs tore through the deli section and the upper body of the worker. Rico was so preoccupied with the deli worker that he didn't notice the young Hispanic man who had crept out of the store's bathroom. The boy blindsided Rico with a broomstick, knocking the gun from his hand. Rico tried to recover the weapon, but was rewarded with a blow to the side of the head that almost knocked him out. Before he knew what was going on, the stock boy had retrieved the Colt and was now aiming it at him.

"El Pogo is gonna pay me top dollar for your thieving ass head," the boy told him, just before his shoulder exploded. With a shocked expression, he collapsed to the ground. As

Cowboy passed him, he popped the kid once more in the face.

"Yo, Cowboy..." Rico began.

"I don't even wanna hear it," Cowboy cut him off. "Lets just get the fuck outta here," he slung the bag over his shoulder and headed for the exit. On the way out, he stopped in front of the young man who had come into the store. Pointing his gun to his head he asked him, "What did you see?"

"Not a mutha fucking thing!" the kid said, with his hands in the air.

"Good answer," Cowboy replied before hitting the street, running.

# SEVEN

**One thing life walking the shadows** had taught Duce was patience. Shortly after speaking with the crack head, Duce found himself a cut and waited. It didn't take long for Marsha to show herself. She came out of the building strolling like she didn't have a care in the world. She was dressed in a pair of pajama pants with her hair wrapped in a scarf so he knew there was no need to follow her. Wherever she was going it wouldn't be far. Marsha was a girl who prided herself on her appearance and wouldn't be caught dead anywhere except the hood dressed like that.

When Marsha rounded the corner Duce slipped into her building. There were a few curious glances from the hustlers applying their trade, but no one questioned him. An icy chill clung to Duce that touched all he passed and common sense told them to give him a wide berth. Forgoing the elevator, Duce bounded the eleven flights of stairs. By the time he got to the top he felt a little winded. Just one more reason he needed to quit smoking. He found Marsha's door with little to no effort. He and his brother had spent many a night at Marsha's talking about their plans for the future. Those days were long gone and this visit was anything but a social one.

Placing an ear and the palm of his hand to the door, Duce checked for signs. There was no vibration, which would come from people moving around, and the only sound was that of the television, which had been left on a video channel. As he could tell, no one was inside. From within his pocket he produced a small case containing what he needed to get into the house.

For all the money Scott was supposed to be getting in the streets, he could've at least made sure Marsha had better locks. It took all of 30 seconds for Duce to gain entry into the apartment. Pistol in hand, he crept into the house, alert for signs of danger. The first place Duce checked was the bedroom. The king-sized bed was freshly made with red satin sheets, while scented candles were placed on both night stands. Apparently Marsha had a romantic evening with her baby daddy planned, but Duce would change all that. His mouth literally watered at the thought of getting Marsha and Scott at the same time.

Along the wall leading back to the living room, there were pictures of Marsha and her son over the years. From what Duce assumed was the most recent pictures, the boy looked to be about four or five. His guess was that Marsha had probably gotten pregnant by Scott just before or immediately after Knowledge's murder. "Death before dishonor," Duce mumbled as he casually knocked the picture to the ground, shattering the image.

Marsha's crib was ghetto fabulous. There was nice furniture and a plasma television hanging from the wall, but the place looked like it hadn't been cleaned in days. Clothes were scattered across the living room floor and something he couldn't identify was marinating in a bowl on the coffee table. Mess aside, her shit was plush, but not as fly as when Knowledge was hitting it. This left the lingering question of *why*? The whole situation was twisted. Marsha used to be his brother's heart, his rider. What could a shit-bird like Scott have offered her to make her betray a stand up nigga like

Knowledge? Duce had an abundance of questions, but it was the thirst for blood that moved him. Duce ignored the mess that was her living room and made his way over to an arm chair, where he settled in and waited for Marsha to come back.

Marsha was feeling herself when she stepped off the elevator with Tic in tow. He was a lean, dark-skinned cat with hazel nut eyes. Tic was doing his thing down in the Jefferson projects, with a team of young thoroughbred niggaz. Though he wasn't a boss just yet, the boy had star potential written all over him. Marsha had had her eye on him for a minute, but tonight would be the first night she let him taste her love.

She had been planning the turnout for a week so the whole thing was laid out from A to B. Scott had been avoiding her crib like the plague since the warrant squad had come around looking for him, so the chances of him coming by without calling were slim to none. Still to that day he hadn't figured out how they'd tracked him to Marsha's address, and had you told him he still probably wouldn't have believed that she was behind it. She didn't want him in jail, but she needed a little space to do her. Scott kept her laced because they had a child together, but he really wasn't *husband* material. The only bitch he loved was the streets and Marsha was cool with that, so long as she had what she needed for her and hers.

Marsha slipped her key in the door and stepped into the apartment. As soon as the door closed, Tic was on her. He pressed his lips to hers and tried to jam is tongue down her throat. She reciprocated by massaging his penis through his jeans until it was rock hard. Marsha was pleased at what she felt. Never breaking the lip-lock, they backed into the darkened living room. Marsha was just about to rip his jeans open and bless him when Tic abruptly stopped.

"What's wrong, baby?" she spoke into his ear.

"Sup, baby girl?" Duce's icy voice floated across the room. Marsha felt the blood draw from her face even before she turned around and saw Duce with a pistol pointed in her direction. "That doesn't look like ya baby daddy."

They told her he would never see the streets again.

"D-Murder is going to spend the rest of his life in jail," that was the promise she'd been made for her part in Knowledge's murder, and here he was…in her house. Marsha wanted to faint, but her body had become paralyzed with fear.

"Fuck is going on?" Tic pushed away from Marsha.

Duce clicked on the small lamp, illuminating the side of his face. The weak light played tricks with his features giving him a demonic appearance. "Just a little unfinished family business."

"Oh my God," Marsha gasped.

"Damn, only five years and you already forgot my name?"

"Duce…"

"Bitch," he cut her off, "that name is for family and you lost that security blanket when you started lying with snakes. No offense, money," he said to Tic.

"My dude, I don't know what the fuck is going on, but it ain't got shit to do with me," Tic tried to bargain.

Duce took on a very sincere tone. "Sadly you don't, but unfortunately this bitch has got you in a jam, son. Marsha," he kicked one of the wooden dining room chairs over to her, "why don't you have a seat, boo."

It was a good thing he had slid the chair over to her because Marsha felt like her knees were going to give out on her at any second. Taking the seat she turned her terrified eyes to Duce. "D, why you feel like you gotta bring a gun into my house? You know me," Marsha said in a shaky voice.

He shook his head. "Nah, I don't know you. I know the mutha fucka you pretended to be when you were with my brother. The bitch I knew would've never betrayed the fam."

"D, I swear on my kids I ain't have nothing to do with what happened to Knowledge."

In the breath of a second after the lie left her mouth, Duce's leg shot out and kicked the chair from beneath Marsha. She crashed to the ground, banging her head on the hard project floor. By the time Tic moved, Duce was kneeling in front of him with the nine pointed at his crotch. Even if he hadn't shaken his head, Tic knew better than to stir.

"Let's try this again," Duce said, getting to his feet slowly. "Help ya bitch up," Duce shoved Tic roughly, "so we can get this show on the road."

Not knowing what else to do, Tic helped Marsha to her feet and back into the chair. Though her eyes pleaded for him to believe that she had nothing to do with what was going down, he didn't believe her. If he was lucky enough to live through the ordeal he would settle up with her real ugly.

"Why, Marsha?" Duce began. "My brother loved you and you fed him to the dogs, help me to understand this shit?"

"D, I know what you think went down, but it wasn't like that," Marsha sobbed. "Knowledge was out here fucking everything on two legs, so it was only natural that I did my thing. Scott was just a young nigga with some good dick; my heart always belonged to Knowledge."

"So much so that you started playing house with one of his killers? Marsha, you know better than to bullshit me," he stepped into the space between Marsha and Tic. "My brother was one of the kindest niggaz to ever play the game, and he's gone because a hating ass nigga wanted his spot."

"D, I didn't know they were gonna kill Knowledge, you gotta believe me."

"The only thing I believe is that my brother is dead,

and he's gonna need some company in hell," Duce spat. "Where's that sneaky ass nigga Scott?"

"I don't know. He comes and goes as he pleases," she said.

Duce placed his gun to the back of her head. "Bitch you better tell me something that's gonna keep your brains from fucking up this nice ass living room set."

"I don't know!"

Duce sighed. "Somehow I don't believe you."

BANG!

Cowboy and Rico were headed north up Broadway while the police were flying south. They had beat the heat by less that three minutes and Cowboy thanked the Thief Gods above that he had made it out on time. Rico hadn't shut his mouth since they had left the bodega. He was so busy talking that he hadn't even known they'd left the city until they were passing the sign for Patterson, N.J.

"Yo, kid, fuck we doing in Jersey?" Rico asked, looking at the unfamiliar surroundings.

"What, we gonna hang out in Harlem after ripping El Pogo off?" Cowboy asked. "We gotta get low for a minute. I got a bitch that stay out in Elizabeth, so we can crash at her pad until the morning."

"Cowboy you always got shit figured out, son!" Rico said.

"For sho, my nigga," Cowboy coasted the car to the side of the road and pulled over. When they had come to a full stop, he killed the head lights. "I gotta take a leak," he said, stepping out of the car.

"Yeah, I gotta squeeze the melons too." Rico got out on the passenger side and went to stand beside Cowboy, who was relieving himself on the side of the road. "Yo Cowboy, good looking out on saving my life back there, kid. Yo, shorty was gonna try to air me out. If I hadn't fucked around and…" Rico didn't even get to finish his sentence before Cowboy shot him in the side and again in the chest.

"You talk too fucking much," Cowboy said to the corpse, tucking his gun back into his pocket. After giving a quick look around, he hopped back into the vehicle and sped off.

Marsha pissed her pajama pants at the sound of the gunshot. It took almost a full minute for reality to set in and she realized that she was still alive. Looking over at Tic she couldn't say the same. Feathers from his bubble coat were falling softly from the apple sized hole in his chest. Tic's head was cocked at a funny angle in the chair, and his eyes held a far off look in them. Not being able to hold it down, Marsha threw Chinese food up all over the floor.

"Marsha, you gonna tell me something, or the next one is yours." Duce told her.

Marsha thought on it for a minute. Scott had his uses, but she hardly saw him as being worth her life. "Willie's Lounge!" she blurted out. "Scott goes through there a few times a week to get his drink on."

"You bullshitting me?" he tapped the barrel of the gun against her nose.

"That's my word, D. You can catch him in there most nights, I swear on everything, just please don't shoot me," she pleaded.

"Calm down, baby, that's not for you," he touched his cheek gently to hers. "For as fucked up as you are, you still brought my brother a little happiness while he was here," he whispered into her ear. His hand slid to the dining room table and retrieved a steak knife that had been left on a dirty plate, "but you still have to answer for what you've done."

"Derrick," she called him by his first name, praying that it would stir some type of their lost love of long ago. "Please, ain't no body gonna be here for my son. Ain't you got no heart?"

He nuzzled her neck as a lover might've and replied, "My heart died with my brother," before dragging the knife from one side of her throat to the other.

Tito sat on the plush suede recliner, smoking a cigarette like it was the last one on earth. He tried to appear as calm as possible, but the sweat in his palms gave him away. He hated to deliver bad news, especially when the recipient was known to fly off the handle and kill indiscriminately.

Across from him a young woman lounged on the loveseat, taking petite pulls of a blunt of what smelled like pure chronic. One leg was thrown over the arm of the chair revealing just enough thigh to send his mind wondering. He did everything in his power to keep from gazing at the cinnamon thigh, but even had he not been about to break terrible news to his boss, he would've never been foolish enough to covet anything El Pogo owned.

The man of the house appeared beneath the arc of the living room entrance, wearing nothing but a silk robe and flip-flops. El Pogo was thin, with wavy black hair that he usually wore in a ponytail, but that night it hung freely around his angular face. His smoke gray eyes seemed to bore into Tito's very soul, making it hard for him to meet the man's gaze.

"Tito, I know you didn't wake me up in the middle of the night just to sit there with a stupid look on your face," El

Pogo said, in a raspy tone.

"No," Tito began, but couldn't seem to find the words to continue.

"Then tell me, why are you here?"

"El Pogo, I know you hate to hear bad news over the phone so I came to deliver my report personally," he cast a glance at the woman, silently asking if it was okay to talk in front of her.

"Madelina, wait for me in the bedroom. I won't be long," he said to the woman. She gave him an obedient smile and slithered off the couch. On her way to the bedroom, she gave Tito a look that he was hardly foolish enough to acknowledge.

"So," El Pogo took the seat the woman had vacated. "Tell me what troubles you, Tito?"

Tito thought about a diplomatic way to phrase it, but diplomacy wouldn't have done him much good with El Pogo. If he was going to flip, pretty words wouldn't cushion the blow so it was better to just spit it out. "Our store on 147th got robbed."

"Robbed?" though El Pogo's voice remained neutral, the temperature in the room seemed to go up a few degrees. "How the fuck did this happen?"

Taking a breath, Tito went on to explain the situation to El Pogo as it had been explained to him by the crew at the spot. Needless to say, El Pogo was not pleased.

In a flash, El Pogo had a razor in his hand and was pinning Tito by the neck to the recliner. "You mean to say that some little monkey mutha fuckas were able to run up in my spot, make off with twelve and a half kilos of my coke and 65 grand of my money?" El Pogo leaned in so close that spittle hit Tito in the face.

"El Pogo, I had nothing to do with it. I wasn't even in the spot when it happened," Tito gasped.

"I don't give a fuck who was in the spot, it happened on your watch so it's your mess to clean up," El Pogo pressed the razor to Tito's cheek, but didn't cut him. "Tito, you better tell me you've got a lead on these cock suckers or it's your ass in the fire!"

Tito swallowed. "From what Rosa says, there were two of them who took the coke, but one of my look outs says that three men left. He says that two of them he's never seen, but the third one comes in the store from time to time to buy beer and shit so he's probably local."

"I want them, Tito. I want my money, my coke and the sons of bitches that had the balls enough to rob me for it." El Pogo demanded.

"On everything I love, I'll take care of it!" Tito almost shrieked.

"I'm sure you will," El Pogo slacked his grip a bit. "And just to make sure you're properly motivated," El Pogo flicked his wrist and cut Tito's face, not enough to scar him, but enough to draw blood. "Get my shit, Tito, or I'm gonna cut more than your pretty little face," El Pogo patted him on the bloody cheek before leaving Tito to show himself out.

# EIGHT

**Frankie was awakened** by the sounds of Jane's Addiction's *Been Caught Stealing*. Without even looking at her cell she knew who it was so she didn't bother to answer. Just as she was about to drop back off to sleep, her house phone started ringing. She tried to ignore it as she had done her cell, but unlike her cell the house phone's ringer was much louder. The caller obviously wasn't getting the hint so she picked up.

"Hello?" she rasped into the phone.

"Nigga, why you ain't pick up ya cell?" Cowboy barked.

"Good morning to you too," Frankie yawned.

"Frankie, I know you ain't trying to be funny?"

Frankie cast her sleepy eyes to the digital clock, which read 9:30am. "Cowboy, it's too early for this shit."

"Oh, you leave me stranded last night and you got the nerve to have a fucking attitude? What the hell happened to you?"

"Ask ya bitch what happened to me!" Frankie snapped.

"Come on, Frankie, I told you that shit wasn't bout nothing so stop acting like that."

"Wasn't about nothing," she snaked her neck as if he could see her. "Cowboy, how long do you think I'm gonna put up with this shit? You can't keep sticking your dick in these young girls you love so much and running up in me. I respect my body too much to let you keep playing craps with our lives. If you can't be true to me, don't be shit to me."

Cowboy sighed. "Frankie, you know I love you, mommy. Mutha fuckas talk out of jealousy and your overactive imagination always tries to convince you that it's true. On my kids, my heart only beats for Frankie Five-Fingers."

"Cowboy, you can't keep hurting me," she said, half burying her face in the pillow so he couldn't hear the sobs. "One day I'm gonna get fed up and bounce, I swear I am," she tried to force the power of truth into the words, but it wouldn't come. "I'm better than this."

"Hush with that foolishness, baby," he cooed. "I'd rather die a thousand deaths than force one day of misery on you. You're my better half, Frankie Five Fingers and I couldn't go on without your strength," the lies rolled off his tongue so easily that he actually believed them. "I went through with that thing last night."

Frankie's mind immediately switched to *money* mode. "You tried to pull a two man job alone? You fool son of a bitch, you're lucky you didn't get killed!"

"I'm a'ight, but I can't say the same about young Pablo." Pablo was the coded nickname he and Frankie used when talking about Rico.

"How bad was it?" Frankie asked, thinking about the bumbling young boy. She's always liked Rico, but couldn't tolerate his presence.

Cowboy sighed. "No tears in the end, baby," he said, letting her know that there had been bloodshed. "Some niggaz just ain't ready to play at this level. Now, what the hell are you doing?"

"I was sleeping until somebody's ass woke me up." she said, sarcastically. "Fuck are you doing up so early anyway?"

"Got my ear to the ground to see what I hear."

"You think homeboy is gonna figure the riddle out?" she asked, sounding concerned. Frankie knew the cat that Cowboy had ripped off was far from a slouch and the greatest of care needed to be taken.

"Like I give a shit," he said, arrogantly. "But check it, I need you to get your pretty ass up and get over here."

"Cowboy, I know you don't think I'm gonna get up outta my bed to come over there and give you some pussy, especially before you get your nasty ass tested?"

He ignored her comment and gave a light chuckle. "I got some things I need to drop off with the fat man and I need a reliable set of eyes in the back of my head."

Frankie knew who the fat man was and didn't look forward to being in his presence. "Damn, can't you take Thor or one of them?"

"They are coming, but they're just muscle. I need my ill na-na on my arm," he thought on it for a minute. "Hold on, why am I even explaining this shit to you? I know this ain't my ride or die bitch talking like some square ass broad? Frankie what the fuck has gotten into you?"

"Nothing," she lied. In all truthfulness Frankie had been rattled by what she saw, or what she thought she saw. For as much as she hated to admit it, Cowboy had a point. She wasn't some square as broad, she was a rider on a down ass team. If she didn't work, she didn't eat, and she was allergic to poverty. "What time we rolling?"

"As soon as you get here, so get the lead out, ma."

"A'ight, I'll be there in an hour or so." She was about to end the call, but Cowboy's voice halted her.

"And wear something sexy."

71

Duce felt the presence before he even heard the key jiggle in the lock. Though his brain still felt hazy with sleep, survival instinct willed his body to move. As silent as a cat, he rolled off the couch, grabbing his pistol off the floor where it rested. As the door creaked inward, Duce fought back the urge to act off impulse, and held his position, directly behind it. Only when he could see the intruder's silhouette cast framed in the dim morning light did he take action.

As soon as enough of the intruder's arm was visible, Duce took hold of it about the wrist and pulled inward with all his might. Normally, this move would've thrown an opponent off balance, leaving them at Duce's mercy, but it didn't go down like that. The intruder pushed off the door, throwing himself backward and slamming Duce into the back of the door. Before Duce could compose himself the stranger kicked the door inward, whacking Duce in the forehead. This woke Duce up completely.

Duce heard he familiar sound of steel sliding against leather and managed to move out of the way just before the intruder stuck his arm inside the apartment and popped two shots. Before the intruder could remove his arm Duce kicked the door with all his might, drawing a yell from the intruder, but he still held his gun. Duce locked the intruder's shooting arm between his hip and elbow, twisting the intruder's injured wrist up and out. Instead of the intruder releasing his grip on the gun, as Duce had hoped, he pushed his weight forward sending himself and Duce spilling to the floor. When they landed, Duce was on the bottom with the intruder's pistol pointed at his head.

"Smitty?" Duce looked up in surprise.

"Who the fuck did you think it was?" the older man

asked, still pointing his pistol at Duce's head. "I could've killed your stupid ass!"

"I wouldn't have been going alone," Duce looked down. Smitty followed his eyes and saw that Duce had his own gun trained on Smitty's crotch.

"Still as arrogant as ever," Smitty eased off Duce and helped him to his feet.

"Nigga, stop fronting," Duce said, accepting the hand up. "Fuck are you doing creeping in my spot in the first place?"

"You forget you told me to watch it while you were away?" Smitty dangled the keys Duce had given him before he blew trial.

"My fault, dawg, you know old habits die hard," Duce raised his pistol.

"For as long as your ass is black, don't you ever draw steel on me!" Smitty tossed him the keys, which Duce caught with his free hand. "Now give me a hug, you black mutha fucka!"

Duce smiled and embraced his homey. Smitty was one of the few cats left in the world that Duce could call friend. Back when Duce was still trying to get out from under his brother's shadow, Smitty was laying his gangsta down on the streets of New York. He was only a few years older than Duce, but had a reputation for being one of the hardest cats on the streets. Knowledge had taught Duce everything he knew about the game, but it was Smitty who had turned him on to killing.

When Smitty was on his game, he and Duce loomed over Knowledge like two avenging angels. With Butch as his advisor and the two killers shadowing him, Knowledge's rule over the block was undisputed, but tragedy had broken up the quartet even before Duce had gone away. One summer night a crew of young bucks who had been sent by a rival came to kill Smitty. They caught him coming out of the supermarket with his wife and aired his car out. Smitty took six, which landed him in a coma for weeks, but he was luckier than his wife had been. One shot had sent her to her final reward. Duce had personally tracked the killers and executed them in a horrible fashion, but Smitty never recovered from the loss. When he was well enough, he moved his daughter to a small house in Long Island and turned his back on the game for good.

"Man, I almost killed the last friend I got in the world," Duce tucked the burner into the waistband of his jeans. "Why didn't you call before you popped up over here?"

"I did, but you didn't answer your phone," Smitty nodded to the Nextel, which was sitting on the coffee table, dead as Jimmy Hoffa.

"Shit, I forgot to charge it," Duce remembered. "Come on in and have a seat," Duce motioned toward the couch. "Want me to fix you a drink?" Duce asked, heading towards the mini bar in the corner.

"You know my poison," Smitty said, rubbing his sore wrist. "I should kill your simple-minded ass for what you did to my wrist."

"Old man, you ain't killing nothing and you ain't letting nothing die," Duce teased him, while pouring two shots of Jack Daniels.

"I got your old man," Smitty said, brandishing his .44. It was one of the few kinds of guns that he would use. "Man, I didn't even expect you to be here. Ain't you on work release or something?"

"Work release is for niggaz on parole, Smitty. I'm a free man." Duce said, handing him his drink. "Thanks to you. I owe you, big time."

"You don't owe me shit, D. That little bit of work I put in to help spring you could never balance the scales for what you did for me. Not a day goes by when I don't think of her, or see her in Rachel's face. Nah, I owe you." The cold fire in Smitty's eyes seemed to burn away the tears that surely wanted to fall.

Duce placed a hand over Smitty's and looked him square in the eyes. "One of the first things you taught me was that there are no debts between *true* friends." Smitty didn't speak, he just nodded his head. "Speaking of Rachel how is she?"

This got Smitty to smile. "Smelling her ass. Ever since she hit thirteen she thinks that qualifies her as a woman."

"Damn, Rachel is thirteen?" Duce said, still thinking of her as the sassy eight year old he'd left.

"Yeah, man. Even got little tits and shit," he laughed. "I had to chase a lil nigga from round my house the other day."

Now, it was Duce's turn to laugh. "I hear you, but at least living out in Long Island, she ain't gotta deal with the same shit we was going through coming up."

"Duce, we live in a great neighborhood and Rachel goes to a mostly white school, but in every city there's a ghetto. I mean, I try to keep her from around that bullshit, but I know she slips away from time to time. I guess she got it honest, because me and Monica used to tear the streets up something awful."

"Fuck yeah. I remember when that girl slapped me on 115th street. I was gonna stomp the bitch out, but Monica talked me out of it. She said a real man doesn't hit a lady, right before she stomped that bitch damn near into a coma!"

"Yeah, my girl could throw them thangs," Smitty agreed, with a far off look in his eyes.

Duce felt his pain like there was a wire connecting them. "Smitty, I didn't mean to bring her up. Man I…"

"It's cool, man. It's been a long time since I was close

enough to anyone to reminisce on her. A lot of times it's the same thing that's hurting you that helps build immunity to it. I'll never forget Monica, but I know I can't live for the dead. Rachel needs me, so I gotta keep it together," Smitty paused for a minute to gather himself. "Enough about this square shit, D-Murder you ready to come out and play?"

"Ready? Shit he made a grand appearance last night. I went to holla at…"

Smitty raised his hand for silence. "Don't say another word, Duce. You keep that shit between you, God and the devil," Smitty reminded him. Smitty used to always preach the importance of keeping your dirt to yourself. Anybody who could possibly jam you had to go. Duce took Smitty's words as gospel and it was what kept him in the game for so long.

"Yeah, I'm definitely on my job," Duce nodded. "I got some leads to follow up on, but in a hot minute, D-Murder gonna drop the curtain on these faggots."

"Well, I'm ready to boogie when you are. It's been a while since this old dog has tasted blood," Smitty told him.

Duce gave him an affectionate look. "Dawg, as much as I appreciate the offer I can't take you to hell with me. You got a kid and a square life, and I couldn't disrupt that. I'm gonna put all my brother's affairs in order and that's that."

Smitty wanted to protest, but he knew Duce was right. He loved Knowledge and would lie anything down for him, but he had Rachel to think about. He couldn't risk fucking her life up on a five year old vendetta.

"Okay," Smitty nodded. "So you gonna take over Knowledge's old operation after you lay these suckers?"

Duce thought on it for a minute. "Nah, I ain't fucking wit it. After I pull this last joint, I'm out."

"One more lick, huh?" Smitty smiled.

"Yep, one more lick and I'm out of here."

"I can dig it, D. Oh, your ride is downstairs."

This changed Duce's whole demeanor. "Aw shit, you brought my baby!" Duce said excitedly, grabbing his coat off the recliner, where he had thrown it the night before. "I hope my shit ain't all dented up!" he said, leaving the apartment with Smitty in tow.

Duce felt like a kid at Christmas as he took the steps two at a time. The leftover snow that soaked his socks through his slippers didn't even seem to bother him when he sloshed through it coming out of the building. For the last five years the only transportation he had experienced was prison buses. The broad smile on his face melted away when he spotted his ride.

The truck looked nothing like what Duce remembered. Though the Explorer was forest green, it looked more like brown beneath the dust and grime. The tires were still fresh, but looked horrible against the dirt covered rims. He turned his irritated gaze from the truck to Smitty. "You can't be serious?" he folded his arms.

Smitty shrugged. "You asked me to store it, not clean it."

# NINE

**When the brute known as Thor** stepped from the Escalade, you could almost hear the shocks give a prayer of thanks. Standing well over six feet and built like an offensive lineman, Thor was an intimidating sight with a sadistic streak adding credibility to his rep. The puffy North Face he wore served in concealing the .357 holstered under his arm, but was barely able to cover the handle of his trademark sledge hammer. The four foot combination of steel and wood had put in almost as much work as his massive hands.

Next to step from the vehicle was Cos, or the Colonel as he was sometimes referred to. He had a squared face, which always seemed to be half smiling, but the eyes of a man who had spent most of his life behind the concrete walls of New York State's finest correctional facilities. The full length wool coat and khaki pants gave him the appearance of a business man, and the Mac-11 slung across his chest satisfied all curiosities as to what kind of business he was in. These two men served as Cowboy's enforcers, and when needed, executioners.

Cowboy stepped from the truck decked out in a black turtle neck and black leather jacket. His skull cap was cocked to the side and pulled to the edge of his blacked-out sun glasses. In one hand he held a chrome briefcase and in the other he held a Blackberry, which he couldn't seem to stop fumbling with. Cowboy was still a novice at working the phone, but he felt it made him look intellectual.

Bringing up the rear was Frankie Five Fingers, the avenging angel. As Cowboy suggested, she was dressed seductively, with a low cut burgundy blouse that showed her ample cleavage and skin-tight jeans tucked into a pair of burgundy riding boots. Her hair hung loose, crowning her face, with the bang tickling the tops of her cranberry Gucci shades. Adjusting the fashionable leather knapsack, she did her model strut over to her man.

"Picture perfect," Cowboy said, kissing her cranberry painted lips, careful not to smear the lipstick.

"Not in front of the help," she teased, running her tongue over Cowboy's lips. She nicked his bottom lip to let him know all was not forgiven from their argument.

"I got your fucking *help*," Thor grumbled.

"You know I love you, baby," Frankie stood on her tip-toes and kissed him on the cheek.

"Enough of that," Cowboy pulled her closer to him. "Get your own bitch, nigga, and keep ya mitts off mine," he said playfully to Thor. "Look, y'all be on point. We gonna go in here and handle business with the fat man then we out, dig it?"

"Cowboy, stop acting like we new to this," Cos said, pulling his coat closed at the neck. The icy wind was especially brutal that afternoon. "Handle ya business, fam. If they try any funny business, just be sure to duck because we don't believe in nothing but head shots!" he gave Thor a pound.

"Just be on point," Cowboy said, leading Frankie towards the front of the bar.

Hades was a low key Goth bar located just off West Broadway in the Village. It was a place where the children of the night came to play and chase their troubles in booze, but what most didn't know was that it was a base of operations for a Harlem coke dealer named Butch. At that hour of the day it was nearly empty, but there were a few lost souls hunched over the bar whispering into half empty glasses. When Cowboy and Frankie entered the spot, they were greeted by a shapely hostess who looked like she wasn't getting enough sun.

"Table for two?" she asked, flashing a perfectly white smile, behind blood red lipstick.

Cowboy spoke to her, but his eyes were on her large breasts. "Actually, no. We have an appointment with Mr. Zappa. Tell him that Charles Lagerfeld is here." He gave her a bogus name that Butch would recognize.

"Very well, Mr. Lagerfeld, I'll tell Mr. Zappa you're here. In the meantime, you're welcome to wait at the bar and have a drink, on the house of course," she said in a very friendly manner.

"We'll pass on the drink, thank you." Frankie's voice wasn't hostile, but there was definitely an edge to it. The hostess caught the hint and left without another word. "Don't try me, Cowboy," she whispered to her lover.

"Frankie, your ass is tripping." Cowboy tried to down play it.

"When I start tripping, you'll know about it."

A minute or two later the hostess came back out. She was still wearing her business-like smile, but made it a point not to look at Cowboy for too long. "Mr. Zappa will see you now. If you guys will just follow me," the hostess led them through the maze of tables and passed the bathrooms to a door marked PRIVATE. She tapped on the door twice before pushing it open and stepped back for Cowboy and Frankie to enter. As Cowboy passed, she rubbed her breasts against his arm but Frankie didn't catch it. Sitting behind a modest desk was Mr. Zappa.

Lawrence Zappa, known as Butch on the streets of Harlem, had the mindset of the old regime with a young boy's cunning. Over the 40 something years Butch had been alive he'd seen the birth of several of Harlem's Dons and their untimely demises. One by one they had come and gone, yet Butch remained. Largely in part because the same codes that the Dons had abided by held no place in Butch's heart. To him the only law was survival of the fittest and he exercised that quite often. Butch had been putting in work on the streets since days before Cowboy or Frankie was alive, and continued to thrive. He was a silent partner at Hades, owned three laundry mats, and was still elbow deep in the coke game, which is what brought Cowboy to his doorstep.

"Thank you, Iris," Butch nodded to the young lady, signaling she should leave.

"I'll be outside if you need me, Mr. Zappa," she grinned and backed out of the room.

"Mr. Zappa," Cowboy mock bowed.

Butch gave him a comical look from across the desk. "Cowboy, I know you ain't come all the way down here to fuck with me? Get up, fool!"

"What's good, Butch?" Cowboy righted himself and extended his hand, which Butch pumped jovially.

"Out here trying to get a dollar, same as everybody else." Butch's beady eyes slid over to Frankie and openly admired her outfit. "Five Fingers," he said in a seductive tone, "good to see you, baby girl."

"Lawrence," she said flatly. Normally Frankie kept her personal feelings out of it when it came to money, but Butch repulsed her. Not because he was a pervert, but because she knew first hand his take on loyalty. They had a history dating back to when Knowledge was the boss and Butch was the old head helping hold it together, so she knew what time it was where Butch was concerned. He was a larcenous man, who couldn't be trusted further than you could throw him with one hand. She didn't like him and she wore it on her sleeve.

The only thing that revealed the fact that Butch felt slighted was the glint in his eyes, because his face remained smiling. "Still the coldest young chick on the streets, huh?"

"Ice cold, baby."

"Sho ya right," Butch clapped his hands like she had just sunk a playoff winning shot. "Niceties aside, what you got for me Cowboy?"

"Baby boy, I hold in my hands a very white Christmas, going for a clearance price," he patted the case. "You know I ain't no drug dealer, so I brought it to someone I know who could benefit from it." He dropped the case and spun it around so it would open towards Butch.

Butch carefully undid the latches, keeping an eye on Cowboy and Frankie. Though they were friends, for whatever that meant in the drug game, he knew just how underhanded Cowboy was and would be damned if they'd have a repeat performance of five years prior. Once the case was open, Butch took a moment to examine its contents.

"Whoo-wee, what do we have here?" Butch rummaged through packages. "Damn, C, this about four keys right there."

"Four and a quarter," Cowboy corrected. "The quarter is on the house my nigga, as a show of good faith. Long story short, I got eight and three quarters more where that came from, and I'm gonna give you a big time play cause you my nigga."

Butch gave him a suspicious look. "And how much of a play are you gonna set em out for, *my nigga*?"

Cowboy ran his fingers across the modern stainless steel desk. "Well, I know you're probably getting them at about 28, maybe 27, depending on the conditions and quality…. So let's say I give you this high grade shit at about 22 a smash?

"Twenty-two, huh?" Butch hauled his nearly 400 pound frame up from his chair and waddled around the desk to the two seats Frankie and Cowboy occupied. Placing a hand on the backs of both their chairs, he continued. "Even if the going rate was $27,000, you're letting them go for five grand cheaper than their worth on the street. To what do I owe this act of good faith?"

Cowboy shrugged, but didn't bother to turn around to where Butch was standing. He wasn't worried about Butch doing anything stupid, because even though he wasn't strapped, Frankie was. "Like I said, I'm no drug dealer."

"No, but you're a hustler and I think you're trying to hustle me," Butch rested his hand on Frankie's shoulder, which she slapped away. "You know, it's funny but I just heard this morning that El Pogo got ripped off for a couple of keys and then a non-drug dealer, but notorious thief, shows up on my doorstep with kilos to sell at a few stacks under the normal clip. Am I reaching here, *my nigga?*"

Cowboy glared up at him while tapping his pack of cigarettes against his hand. "Butch," Cowboy slid a cigarette out of the pack and placed it in his mouth, "ain't no shame in what I do and anybody you ask will tell you the same. This coke don't know where it came from, same as the money don't know where it's going," Cowboy lit the cigarette. He took a deep pull, savoring the stale taste of the cancer stick. "At the end of the day, business is business, baby."

Butch silently stared at Cowboy, and the young robber matched his look. "Cowboy, I almost forgot how much of a bastard you were."

Cowboy looked at him seriously. "Most people do, and that's why it's so easy for me to catch a mutha fucka slipping. But you know just as much about treachery as I do, right? Old ghosts aside though, you ain't the only stop on my route, so let me know something?"

"A'ight, fam, you know I fucks wit you. But let me get them joints at eighteen a clip. You know I gotta move em slow so their previous owners don't get the wrong idea," Butch bargained.

Frankie glared at Butch, but held her tongue, letting Cowboy handle his business. "Man, 22 is a stick up, but you determined to fuck me with no Vaseline? Dawg, I can get 25 out in the Stuy, but I come to you cause you my man. And since you my man I can go twenty-one-five, but anything shorter and I gotta bounce."

Butch wandered back around the desk and re-took his seat. Frankie was ice grilling him, but he was focused on Cowboy. The smug way the young man looked at him made Butch tight, but he was too seasoned to show it. He knew that was El Pogo's coke that Cowboy was selling, therefore, the quality was on time and the price was more than right. Did he really wanna let Cowboy walk out of there with it over a few dollars?

"A'ight G," Butch reached for a desk drawer and Frankie was on her feet with the .380 pointed at his face. "Easy, baby," he said, freezing in place. "I'm just reaching for the bread," only when Cowboy gave her the nod did Frankie lower her gun. Slowly Butch began pulling stacks of money from the drawer and placing them on the desk. When he was done, there was $86,000 lying on the table which he pushed over to Cowboy. "Imma take these for now. Tomorrow I'll send somebody over to pick up the rest."

"See, I knew we could come to an understanding," Cowboy admired the money. The sound of the door opening startled him and spun Frankie, but the tension faded when Iris entered the room. Frankie eyed her cautiously as she placed two extra large takeout bags on the table baring the Hades logo. Without so much as a second look, Iris turned and left the way she came.

Butch smiled easily. "I know you didn't plan on carrying all that cabbage in your pockets?"

"I trust everything went well," Cos said from the passenger seat of the truck. He had a blunt dangling in between his lips and his lighter poised for action.

"Smooth as silk, baby boy," Cowboy patted the shopping bag on his lap; Frankie was holding the other one.

"You're about a lucky son of a bitch," Thor added, from his position behind the wheel.

"It ain't got nothing to do with luck, this shit is pure skill!" Cowboy boasted.

"Stupidity is more like it. Man, what was you thinking when you jacked El Pogo?" Cos asked.

"I was thinking he had that bread and how sweet it is," Cowboy said honestly. "Cos, I knew you was gonna trip on it, so I had to go lone wolf. What's done is done, so fuck talking about it. All I wanna know is are y'all down to celebrate tonight?"

"You know I'm always down for a party," Thor said.

"Yeah, man. We can hit the spots and get shit faced. How's that sound to you?" Cowboy asked Frankie.

"Been there done that," she said, thumbing through the bills. "Ya'll do the guy thing, I'm probably gonna hook up with Mo."

"If you like it, I love it," Cowboy said, secretly thinking of the pussy he could get while Frankie was gone. "Cos, why don't you bring the young boy out tonight? I wanna feel him out before we do the Doll House."

"I still can't believe y'all letting an outsider into our thing. You better hope he don't turn out to be no snitch,"

Frankie warned.

"Nah, homey is a straight shooter. I seen his paperwork, and the boy was in the street handling before he got
knocked. Even the bulls steered clear of that cat on the yard."

"I don't give a fuck what he did on the yard. I'm more
worried about how he handles himself on the street."

"We'll see what he's made of," Cos said, finally lighting the blunt.

# TEN

**Tito paced the dim living room** replaying the robbery in his head. He watched so much C.S.I. and Law and Order that he considered himself somewhat of an expert. On a glass table, under a reading lamp were the remains of the plastic restraints and a beat up bullet. Mustache had screamed like a girl when the old woman cut it out, but they couldn't risk him going to the doctor.

Tito thumbed one of the plastic restraints. "Definitely someone who does this," he said to no one in particular. Even before he had examined the evidence, he knew whoever had hit El Pogo's bodega wasn't a novice. Only a real ballsy or real skilled thief could've gotten away with it, and he figured the leader was a combination of both.

Still thumbing the restraint, Tito headed down the hall to the bathroom. There was a man standing outside the door looking on while another man spoke quietly to a young boy who was slumped on the toilet. It had taken them no time at all to find the third black who had been in the bodega. Kids like him never strayed too far from what was familiar to them so it was just a matter of playing the block and waiting. Once they had him under wraps Tito began the interrogation, which had been violent and unpleasant.

"You ready to talk to me now?" Tito asked, glaring

down at the boy. His lips were split and bleeding, while the left side of his face looked like chopped meat.

The kid was visibly dazed, looking around trying to locate the voice. When his puffed eye landed on Tito, he tensed. "Man, I swear on my dead grandmother's grave I ain't have shit to do with that robbery!" he sobbed.

"So it was by accident that you were seen coming out of the bodega right after it happened?" Tito slapped him. "Don't play with me, monkey!"

"Yo, God, I was just going into the store to get some blunts and these niggaz was like shooting shit up. I just got low and tried to wait it out, that's my word!"

Tito picked up a wilted newspaper that had been sitting on the floor. It was splotched with blood, but the headline was still legible: *Harlem Youth Found Shot to Death Outside Fort Lee, New Jersey*. The actual words were smeared, but it was the picture of the victim that Tito was more interested in. From what they had learned from the kid so far, the dead man was the accomplice. Apparently, whoever had master-minded the robbery wasn't leaving any loose ends.

"Looks like your boy is killing off anyone who could finger him in the robbery," Tito said, literally shoving the newspaper into the kid's face. "If we hadn't gotten to you, he surely would have."

"I don't know neither one of them cats," the kid shook his head violently.

Tito looked at the man who had been whispering to the kid when he came in, but the man just shrugged. "He's been kicking the same shit for the last half hour. I don't think he's gonna rat on his homeboys, T."

Tito stared at the pleading look in the boy's eyes. "Shoot him and let's get out of here," Tito said, turning to leave the bathroom.

"Cowboy!" the kid blurted out.

Tito stopped and turned slowly. "What did you say?"

"Cowboy," the kid choked on his tears. "The dead guy from the newspaper called the other one Cowboy, but man, that's all I know."

Tito looked at Whisper to see if the name rang a bell with him. "Ain't that the black dude who be on the motorcycle? You know… the bandito."

Tito wasn't familiar with Cowboy, but he was familiar with his exploits. He was known through out the streets as "The Bandit King", a man with the balls and the brains to take off any caper. Tito vowed that this would be the last caper he took off once they caught up with him. In his mind, he was already thinking of ways they might possibly trap the arrogant little thief.

"You did good, little monkey. Whisper," he turned to the interrogator. "Get that sneaky ass nigga Booby on the case. I wanna know where this Cowboy is at all times. Let's go," Tito said to his two soldiers.

"What about him," Whisper nodded towards the boy who had the hope of survival in his eyes.

"Smoke that little nigger," Tito said wickedly, leaving them to their work.

There was a good amount of traffic on the block that night. Even with the frigid temperature the crack heads ventured out to get their blasts. Both sides of the street were buzzing with traffic as the fiends shuffled back and forth like the walking dead. The corner boys moved everything from nickels to twenties in the still of the December night.

Willie's Lounge sported its normal mix of drunks, macks and sack chasers decorating the curb and entrance. Stumbling out of the bar was the so-called "lynchpin" of the block, Scott. Scott had never been much in the way of a leader, but he was good at taking other nigga's scraps and making something out of them. A few years prior, he had struck a bargain that was supposed to make him a star player in the game. Alas, when the shit hit the fan he was left with a few ounces of coke, a corner of his own, and a badly burned bridge. Still, he made the best out of it, flipping the coke and building clientele. Though he was still low on the food chain, Butch made sure he made enough to keep himself afloat which was acceptable to a nigga like Scott.

Wind whipped through the block sending a swirl of trash into the air. Scott pulled up the collar of his leather jacket to try and deflect some of the wind, but it didn't help. He cursed himself for wearing the stylish, yet thin, jacket knowing it was damn near mid-December, but he wanted to show it off. A chest cold would be the price he paid for fashion.

"How we looking?" Scott asked a slim kid who had come to stand next to him.

"I'm almost done with this pack," the kid replied.

"A'ight, when you're done go get another one from Steve. I'm getting up outta here," Scott told the kid and bounced. Scott had decided that it was too chilly for him to play the block so he decided to turn it in. He had tried to call Marsha again, but she wasn't picking up. She always did that when he stayed out. Their son was at his mother's so there was no telling who or what Marsha was into. Writing her off, he hoped that he could catch one of the lounge stragglers to slide with before the night was done.

Scott made a brief stop at the corner store to grab a cup of coffee and a cigar before stepping out to the curb to flag down a cab. Eighth Avenue wasn't showing him any love so he decided to try his luck on Seventh. Scott made his way down the block sipping his coffee, lost in his own thoughts. A flicker of movement brought him up short. Scott gave a brief look around but other than him, there was no one on the block but two crack heads who were having a minor argument.

"That fucking weed is making me paranoid," he said to the night. Scott kept walking, but he still felt uneasy. Just as he reached the end of the block, he heard a flicking sound. Scott spun and found himself staring at a man huddled in a darkened doorway. The man hadn't done anything or even moved in Scott's direction but the warning alarm in his head was blaring.

The man flicked a lighter and brought it up to his face. The flame played tricks with the light against the man's face, obscuring his features. Though Scott couldn't see him totally, there was something familiar about him. As the man stepped out of the shadows and under the soft glow of the street light, a ball of ice began to form in Scott's stomach. "Oh shit!"

"That wasn't quite the reception that I was expecting," Duce smiled. Scott went for his gun, but Duce beat him to the punch. The 9mm was pointed square between Scott's eyes. "By the time you pull it the fight will be over. Why don't you toss that hammer over here so we can talk?"

Scott thought about trying for it, but he was sure that the man standing before him would shoot him if he did. Hell, he might've shot him if he didn't, but he'd rather try to nego- tiate his way out as opposed to shooting. Scott cursed under his breath and tossed the gun on the ground, with a faint sloshing sound.

"That's better," Duce continued. "It's been a long time, my nigga. Ain't you gonna tell me how happy you are to see me?"

"Truthfully, no, you're the last mutha fucka I ever thought I'd see again," Scott said coldly.

"Nobody did, baby boy, but here I am," Duce spread one arm, but didn't take the gun off Scott. "So what's the good word? I hear you and that fat mutha fucka Butch is out here getting rich, building off the ashes of my brother's shit."

Scott looked into Duce's eyes and could actually feel the hate boring into his face. "D-Murder, I'm just out here trying to eat."

"Eating off the dead? Yeah, I always knew you were a vulture and even a creep, but I'd have never picked you to be a fucking traitor, Scott. That was some slick shit y'all put together though, calling me to the spot with them corpses then tipping the police off to it. Cock sucker, they could've fried me!" Duce took a few steps closer.

"D, don't do nothing crazy. Let's rap about this, fam."

"Nah, we ain't got nothing to talk about. All I want is…" Duce's next word was replaced by a scream as Scott tossed the cup of hot coffee in his face. The liquid was hot enough that it burned when it made contact with Duce's skin, but not enough to leave a mark or deter him from killing Scott. He managed to wipe the sticky black liquid from his eyes just in time to see Scott running top speed back towards Eighth Avenue. If Scott made it out of the block and onto the avenue, it would be harder to kill him because of all the witnesses. No, he had waited too long to let revenge elude him.

Instantly, old muscles came back to life and Duce was after his prey. Scott had too much of a lead on him for Duce to Catch him in an outright sprint so he tried something else. His booted feet made thunderous noises as he ran up the back of someone's Maxima to stand on the roof. The cold mixed with his adrenaline made it hard to breathe, but breathing was essential at that point. Steadying the 9mm in a two-handed grip, Duce jerked the trigger twice.

Scott had managed to make it three buildings from the corner when what felt like a baseball slammed into his shoulder. It happened so fast that Scott didn't even realize that he was shot until he was airborne. His chin made contact with the frosty ground, before the rest of his body did. When he gathered his wits enough to look up, he saw the man he'd known as D-Murder sprinting towards him and began to scream like a frightened child.

"Shut ya bitch ass up," Duce kicked him in the mouth, bloodying his boots. "So, you wanna throw hot coffee on niggaz, huh?" Duce aimed the gun at his face.

"Please, man," Scott pleaded, trying to shield his face with his good arm.

"Huh?" Duce asked as if he didn't hear him. "Are you begging?" he asked sympathetically.

"Listen, I got some dough in the crib. You can have that and my chain if you let me live," he said hurriedly. "Please, man."

"Your chain? Do you think a funky ass chain is gonna bring my brother back?!" Duce fired a bullet into Scott's thigh. A few inches higher and it would've hit him in the testicles. "Let me ask you this," Duce leaned down to whisper to Scott, totally ignoring his screams. "What did you gain from all this, his bitch, and his position? Marsha is a ho and Butch run the block. Fuck you got?"

"D-Murder," Scott called him by his title, hoping the show of respect would increase his chances of living. "Nobody was supposed to die. They said that nothing would change and we'd all be partners if Knowledge would agree to step down, but your brother wasn't trying to hear it. It was supposed to be good for business."

Duce's body went rigid for a moment, but the rage leaked away. "Business," tears glistened in his eyes. "My brother died on a street corner because it was good for business?" Duce fired twice into Scott's gut.

Scott's mouth opened and closed like a beached fish but no sound came out. The pain was so intense that his vocal cords wouldn't work. Duce could've shot him in the head and ended it, but Scott didn't deserve a quick death. He needed to die slow. As Duce looked back and saw Scott trying to keep his intestines from spilling into the snow, he was pretty sure that he would.

Duce drove his Explorer as calmly as he could down St. Nicholas Avenue. There was blood on his boots and a hot pistol on the passenger seat, but panicking wouldn't change that nor would it change the fact that he had killed two people in as many nights. Marsha's death had made him feel better, but he savors Scott's far more. It had been Scott who called Duce to the apartment that would spell his doom, and Scott who he had treated like family. Part of him wanted to turn around and shoot Scott again.

When the Boost phone he'd purchased that day went off, he almost jumped out of his skin. He'd only given one person the number so he knew who it was without looking at the caller ID. "Yo," Duce said, holding the phone with one hand and steering with the other.

"Young blood, what it is?" Cos said.

"Ain't shit, about to go see this broad," Duce lied.

"Man, fuck that broad, I got something better lined up for you. Bring your ass down to 79th and Columbus Ave."

"Come on, Cos, a nigga about to get some ass. You know I'm fresh home," Duce protested. The last thing he felt like doing at that moment was clubbing, especially with all the dirt he was riding with. All Duce wanted to do was hit the FDR and make it back to Brooklyn without incident.

"Fuck that, there's a gang of bitches up in here. Some-body's gonna give your young ass some pussy. Besides, the big homey wants to meet you. We'll be expecting you in about an hour," Cos said, before ending the call.

Duce cursed and tossed the phone roughly into the passenger seat. Meeting Cowboy wasn't something he had planned on just yet, it was messing with the natural order of his plan and Duce hated that, but it was a necessary evil. He knew Cowboy by reputation, but had yet to feel the man out. A good hunter was always familiar with the scent of his prey before the kill.

# ELEVEN

**Booby was huddled so deep in the doorway** of the closed wireless store that you couldn't see him unless you knew where to look. Ever since he was a kid, it had always been easy for him to blend in, or be overlooked, which is what made him such a valuable informant for some of the under world's top figures. That night, he was in the employment of El Pogo, through Tito.

It wasn't hard for him to locate and track his mark, because they were from the same neighborhood. Cowboy had a residence in the middle class complex of Espinard Gardens, while Booby resided on 147$^{th}$ and Seventh. He knew what Cowboy and his crew were capable of so he was apprehensive at first, but when he heard how much he'd be paid, it was a done deal. He wasn't sure what Cowboy had done to piss El Pogo off and truthfully he didn't care, as long as he got his cake.

It had been about fifteen minutes since Cowboy and his entourage had entered the bar. When he was sure that they weren't going anywhere, he picked up the phone and dialed the number Tito had given him.

Duce had driven pass the bar twice before he finally spotted it. It was a very nondescript spot located at the basement level of a restaurant. As luck would have it, he was able to park right in front, which was amazing considering the parking situation in New York City. Though he still had on the thermal shirt and jeans at least he was able to find a pair of dusty black Timberlands in the back of the truck. They weren't exactly club worthy, but at least they didn't have blood all over them. Securing his gun under the driver's seat of his truck, he made his way towards the bar.

"Fam, we got a dress code here," the bouncer said before Duce had made it all the way to the descending stairs.

"My dude, I'm fresh off the road just trying to catch a quick drink," Duce said pleasantly.

The bouncer looked him up and down. "Still, the rules are the rules. You can't get in dressed like that."

"Jimmy for as well as we tip your ass I know you ain't out here hassling a member of my team?" A voice floated from the bottom of the stairs. Cos was leaning against a table smoking a cigarette.

"My fault, Cos. I ain't know homey was here with y'all," the bouncer said humbly.

"Well now you do," Cos said, handing him a $50 dollar bill. "Now move your big ass out the way and let my man in."

"What da deal?" Duce stepped passed the bouncer and embraced Cos.

"Welcome home, kid," Cos patted Duce on the back. "How does it feel?"

"Damn good," Duce eyed a scantily dressed young lady who was making her way down the steps.

"Man it's a hundred more like her in the club. Come on down so I can introduce you to the team."

Cos led Duce down the stairs and through two large

wooden doors. The interior of the club was nothing like the quiet exterior. The music was loud, the air was stale and liquor flowed by the gallons. Cos bumped through the crowd passing out handshakes and hugs while Duce followed closely behind. His eyes were constantly scanning the place for trouble. Granted he had never been one to do the nightlife so his face wasn't a familiar one, but you never knew who you'd bump into with the world being so small. The last thing he needed was for someone to recognize him and blow his cover.

They made their way across the bar area to the where the dance floor was located. People of all races were drinking, laughing and grinding to various hits spun by the D.J. A shapely young white girl tried to grab Duce's hand and pull him onto the dance floor, but he politely declined. For as much as he needed to release that five year nut, business always came first. As they approached the far corner of the club, Duce's heart started beating at 100 miles per minute.

There was a brute of a man standing at attention with his eyes sweeping the crowd. The chances of him being armed inside the club was unlikely, but the man looked like he could do some damage with his bare hands. Duce gave him the once over, but his eyes were focused on the man directly behind him. Though Duce had never met the man face to face, he knew the lanky cat dressed in all black had to be Cowboy. He was lounging on the cushioned seat with a pretty redbone on his lap. From his arrogant demeanor and the way he was barking directions at the waitresses you'd have thought he owned the place. He took a minute to stop groping the girl to cast a cold stare up at Duce.

Cos leaned over and spoke to Cowboy. "This is the young boy Duce I was telling you about."

Cowboy eased the young lady off his lap and leaned forward. "So this is the scourge of the New York state prison system? Funny, I expected you to be bigger from all the shit Cos has told me about you."

"I could say the same," Duce returned his glare.

"This is my nigga Thor," Cos said, trying to ease some of the tension. Thor nodded but didn't extend his hand, nor did Duce. "What you drinking on Duce?"

"Vodka and cranberry," Duce said, still eyeballing Cowboy. He knew that Cowboy was testing him and was determined to show the man that he wasn't a punk.

"Come on and cop a squat," Cowboy patted the seat next to him. Duce slid onto the seat, but kept a comfortable distance between himself and Cowboy. "I hear you're looking to come up?"

Duce shrugged. "You know how it is; I'm fresh off a bid and trying to get my ones up."

"I don't know about no ones, but I know that fucking with me you can stack some fifties and hundreds."

"Even better," Duce gave a half smile. "You know, even before I met Cos your name was ringing off in the joint. Everybody from Fishkill to Downstate is talking about the Bandit King," Duce stroked his ego.

"Is that what they're calling me?" Cowboy smiled. "I like that shit. So what else are they saying about me?"

Duce chose his next words carefully. "They say that you're the best friend a guy could have and the worst enemy."

"You better fucking believe it! Me and mine is straight bout that, feel me?"

"No doubt," Duce nodded. "So, my nigga Cos tells me that now that I'm a part of the team I can make some serious paper."

"You ain't part of shit yet, homey. You still gotta prove yourself," Cowboy told him.

"I guess this is the part where you tell me that I gotta kill one of your enemies or go toe to toe with the big man?"

Duce said sarcastically.

Cowboy laughed. "Nah, Thor would murder you in a fight and ain't nobody stupid enough to be my enemy. What I got in mind is something way simpler, but just as dangerous, if you're up to it?"

"Like I told you, I need to get my ones up. I'm down for whatever," Duce said seriously.

"Glad to hear it. Check it, we got this score coming up and this is when you're gonna cut your teeth." Cowboy went on to explain the dynamics of the upcoming robbery while Duce listened intently. Cowboy was a master schemer and every bit of an arrogant Harlem hustler. Had the circumstances been different they might've been able to do business together, but this wasn't the case. Cowboy had violated and had to be served justice, just like the rest of them.

Two hours after arriving at the bar Duce and Cowboy were chopping it up like two old friends. He and Cos were visibly tipsy, from all the drinks they had been throwing back, but not Duce. He sipped with them to break the ice, but he was far from dunk. In his line of work, a split second of indecisiveness could mean the difference between life and death.

Cowboy chatted away while Duce pretended to listen to his ranting. Though he tried to relax, something didn't feel right. His eyes scanned the bar for signs of trouble, but all he could see where the throngs of people on the dance floor, but that didn't remove the eerie feeling in the pit of his gut. Focusing all his senses, he tried to drown out everything around him and zero in on what didn't match in the picture. On his second sweep of the crowd, he spotted the oddities.

Posted against the wall where two Hispanic men. To the untrained eye they looked like two cats just enjoying the scene, but Duce had long ago learned to look beneath the surface of things. The first thing that struck him as odd was the fact that they were standing around in bubble coats in a room where the temperature was 90 something degrees. Even wearing just the thermal Duce was sweating, so he knew they had to be suffering under the goose feathers. Secondly, they weren't drinking. They had drinks in their hands, but the ice had long ago melted out of them and the liquor had yet to be touched. All these things told Duce that something was definitely wrong with the picture, but what sealed the deal were the larcenous glares they were sending over to the corner.

Silently, Duce slid from the seat and headed towards where the bathrooms were located. As he crossed the crowded room, he could feel the eyes of the Hispanics on him, but he didn't look in their direction. Instead of actually going into the bathroom, he pressed himself against the wall which divided the dance floor from the restrooms. He peered around the corner and to his surprise he didn't see the men. A quick scan of the crowd revealed one of them moving in Cowboy's direction, while the other slithered along the wall towards the bathroom.

Duce found himself with one hell of a dilemma. Whoever had set the Hispanic men on Cowboy had nothing to do with him, but Cowboy dying that night wasn't a part of the plan. True, if they killed him it would save Duce the trouble but Cowboy's life was already spoken for. For as much as he hated to do it, he had to take action. Before he had a chance to decide on what to do next, one of the Hispanics rounded the corner with a gun in his hand.

Moving more off instinct than anything else, Duce grabbed the man by his arm and yanked him behind the wall and through the kitchen doors. The kitchen staff screamed and did their best to get out of the way of the two combatants. The Hispanic tried to raise his gun, but Duce had his wrists firmly secured. Being that shooting wasn't an option, he caught Duce with a short left. Duce staggered but kept his grip on the man's wrist. The man tried to swing again, but Duce stepped inside the punch and head-butted him, breaking his nose. With an audible pop, Duce broke the man's wrists sending the gun crashing to the floor. When the Hispanic man tried to lunge for it, Duce caught him in a reverse chokehold. He had only intended on putting the man to sleep, but before he even realized what he was going the man's neck snapped and he went limp in Duce's arms. Ignoring the dead body at his feet, Duce snatched the gun off the floor and headed back to the dance floor.

By the time Duce came around the corner, the other Hispanic man was easing from the crowd and over to Cowboy's group. Thor had his back to the man, still chopping it up with the female, so he never saw the man draw a .45 from his coat. Cos screamed his friend's name before diving out of the line of fire. Cowboy's eyes got as wide as saucers at the sight of the gun, but he was frozen with fear. At the same moment the man made to the pull the trigger, Duce squeezed off.

The shot hit the man in the shoulder, sending goose feathers flying and knocking the man into the D.J. booth, bringing the music to a halt. Duce tried to finish him with the next shot, but ended up blowing the face off a man who was trying to run for cover. Before Duce had a chance to get another shot in, the club was lit up like Christmas. The remaining Hispanic tried to cut Duce down, but ended up shooting the wall as Duce was already on the move. There was too many people running back and forth for Duce to get a clear shot so he had to improvise. Dropping to one knee, he targeted the man's legs. The shot took him off his feet and sat the man on his ass in the corner.

Moving through the crowd with the grace of a jungle cat, Duce eased up on the man who was trying to crawl for the exit. When he saw Duce, he tried to turn the gun on him, but Duce's foot on his hand kept him from raising it.

"That life is spoken for," Duce said, before shooting the man in the face. There was a sudden movement behind Duce, but before he could turn around someone had grabbed him around the waist and lifted him off his feet. He was about to open fire, but stopped when he saw who it was.

"Easy, shotta, we gotta get outta here," Thor said, setting him back on the ground.

Though the monster in Duce longed for more bloodshed, he wasn't willing to run the risk of going back to prison. Wiping the gun thoroughly with his thermal, he tossed it to the ground and followed his team into the night.

# TWELVE

**"That was a close one,"** Cos said, steering the truck onto the Westside Highway.

"Too close. That nigga almost got the drop on me," Cowboy said, while trying to light a cigarette. His hands were shaking so bad that he had to hold the lighter with two hands.

"Good thing Duce was on point," Cos said.

"At least somebody was on point. How the fuck did you let that nigga get up on us?" Cowboy turned to Thor.

"Dawg, I was trying to get laid like everybody else," Thor said.

"Yeah, and you almost got me laid down in the process. If the young boy hadn't let off, I'd be dead right now," Cowboy shot back. He turned to Duce and extended his hand. "Good looking out."

"It wasn't about nothing, man," Duce gave him dap. "If we crew, we gotta look out for each other, right?"

"You ain't a part of this thing yet son," Thor reminded him.

"Thor, stop hating and give the young boy his props. Don't get mad because he did your job better than you," Cos teased him.

"Fuck you, nigga. It's real funny that he was able to

spot them niggaz when the three of us missed them," Thor grumbled.

"Go ahead with that shit, Thor," Cos brushed him off.

"Real talk, Cos. I know this is ya man and all, but I don't trust him. It didn't seem a little strange that he showed up just in time to save Cowboy? For all you know, he could've been the one who sent them spic ass niggaz at us in the first place," Thor accused.

Duce's face became cold. "Man, fuck you! I just save your ass from getting smoked and you gonna come at me sideways? I should slap the shit outta you for even disrespecting me like that."

"Fuck did you say to me, lil nigga," Thor tried to climb over the seat to get to Duce, but Cowboy intervened.

"Cool it, Thor," Cowboy ordered. He turned a suspicious glance at Duce. "Say, how did you know that it was about to go down?"

It felt like everyone in the truck was staring at Duce. If he answered wrong the SUV could very well become his final resting place. Placing his hands on his lap, he looked at the men and spun a brilliant lie. "I knew him from prison."

"What?" all three of them asked in unison.

"Cos, you remember that time you knocked that Blood L.K. nigga out in the library?" Duce asked.

Cos nodded. "Yeah, the little Spanish kid with the scar on his face. I stomped his ass to within an inch of his life. They made me finish my bid in Downstate because of that fight."

Duce grinned as the ends of the lie began to stitch themselves together. "L.K. was setting you up to get done for fucking with one of theirs. The kid I shot was the one they were gonna use. I was coming from the bathroom when I spotted him. I thought they were coming for you, because of the beef, I had no idea he was about to pop Cowboy."

Cowboy studied Duce's face for a long while. Duce initially thought he saw through the lie and was about to make his move, but he relaxed when Cowboy bust out laughing. "Cos," he tapped his partner, "I owe you a bottle. If you hadn't beat that L.K. nigga up, Duce wouldn't have recognized the shooter and I'd be dead. That's some real six degrees of separation shit right there."

"I'm glad you think the fact that a nigga tried to body you is funny," Thor snapped. "Instead of making jokes we need to find out who sent them niggaz and why? What's your little crystal ball say about this one, Duce," Thor mocked him.

"I got a ball for you, two of them actually," Duce grabbed his crotch.

"Why don't the both of you niggaz shut the fuck up!" Cos snapped, finally tired of Duce and Thor's bickering. "Cowboy, this shit looks like a professional job gone wrong. I don't know who you put on to that lil piece of business uptown, but it looks like the chickens are coming home to roost."

"You think El…" Thor began, but Cowboy cut him off.

"Watch your mouth," Cowboy said to Thor, but was cutting his eyes at Duce. Duce pretended not to catch their meaning, but he knew what time it was. The word was all over the streets that El Pogo got ripped off, and the pieces just fell into place as to who had pulled the caper. He tucked that little piece of information in the back of his mind to use at a later date.

Thor grumbled something no one quite understood and continued. "All I'm saying is that it's very possible that they were his men, and if that's the case we've got a hell of a problem on our hands."

Cos nodded in agreement. "The big man has got a point. Homey's got an army and long bread. If he decides to send the wolves at us then we need to think about what we're gonna do."

Cowboy was cool when he addressed his crew. "For now, we try to avoid him, but if he steps wrong then we blow him and his whole crew off the map."

An eerie silence filled the truck as those who knew El Pogo weighed their chances of coming out on top after going to war with him. Finally, it was Duce who broke the silence. "Man, I don't know who this nigga is," he lied, "but if he gotta be got, so be it. I'm wit you, Cowboy."

"Ain't that touching," Thor grumbled.

"Man, you gonna quit questioning my authenticity. When it's time to bang, believe I'm gonna bang," Duce assured him.

"Slow down, partner," Cowboy told Duce. "I see you react quick in the face of bull shit and it's an endearing quality, but never think that because we show you love that you have an opinion in this. You've yet to walk through the fire, my nigga."

"Cowboy, I ain't no bull shit ass nigga. When it's work to be done, I gets it in. Ask around about me. I ain't trying to step on nobody's toes, but I want y'all to know that I'm with you. I was sitting niggaz down in the joint for free, so breaking a mutha fucka up for a few ones on the street is nothing, feel me?"

"Yeah, I feel you, but I still don't know you," Cowboy said. "You an anxious young nigga and that can either make you rich or send the both of us to prison."

"Dawg, I'm just trying to get about mine. I'm fresh out the can with no family and no ends. I'm just trying to get in where I fit in."

Cowboy reclined. "We'll see if you fit in when we hook up to handle that business. I run a tight ship Duce, and every one of us are each other's crutch." Cowboy pulled his gun from under the seat and placed it on his lap, with the barrel facing Duce. "After we snatch your virginity, you're either gonna be a solid member of the family, or one of the whores we cast to the side. The ball is in your court, kid."

The sounds of Alicia Keys' *Unbreakable* floated softly from the wall mounted speakers. You could smell the faint traces of the Black Diamond incense burning in the corner, over an ash catcher, but it was outmatched by the sweet sting of Purple Haze. Mo was propped against the pillows at the head of Frankie's king-sized bed, with a crown of smoke billowing around her head, while Frankie was propped on one elbow at the foot. Frankie could almost feel the strangulating smoke in her throat and for as bad as she wanted to reach for the blunt, she remembered her declaration from earlier.

"This bitch goes in," Mo said, rocking from side to side, mouthing along with Alicia. "Ike and Tina, mutha fucka, Florida and James, that's what the fuck love was about," Mo hoisted her plastic cup, nearly spilling the Nut Cracker on Frankie's bed spread, but like the seasoned drunk she was, not a drop made it over the lip of the cup.

"Bitch, your ass is drunk," Frankie said, taking petite sips through her straw. Unlike Mo, she wasn't big on Nut Crackers, but the fruity drink was quick and to the point when you wanted to go there, and with all that Frankie was going through she *definitely* needed to be there.

"Oh, I'm nice as hell, but I'd need at least two more of these to classify me as drunk," Mo informed her, finishing off what was left in her cup. "I'm just telling my truth, ma. You can't front like Alicia don't go there. Between her, Mary and Keyshia, them broads can tell you about the heartache and triumphs of love."

"Heartache," Frankie chuckled. "I could give all three

of them a run for their money in that department."

Mo rolled down to the foot of the bed and placed her head on Frankie's lap. One look into Frankie's sad eyes and Mo's buzz began to fade. "What's the matter, honey, Cowboy still acting like he doesn't know he's got a diamond?"

Frankie turned her head and blinked away the moisture trying to form in her eyes. "Please, that ignorant nigga ain't never gonna get it right. Cowboy is gonna be who he is, and I ain't really trying to lose no more sleep over that. Sometimes you gotta let a man be who he's gonna be."

Mo slit her eyes. "Frankie, is that man putting roots on you?"

"No, simple-minded ass, there's nobody putting roots on me," she was smiling, but her eyes were still sad. "I just understand that you can't control a man's actions. They've either gotta be true, or not, simple as that."

Mo sat up and looked down at her friend. "Baby girl, that's the biggest lie you've ever told. Frankie, you've been my ace bitch for as long as I can remember, but ain't none of this game rubbed off on you yet? This here," she patted her crotch, "makes us Goddess amongst men, provided we know what to do with our gifts. Sweetie, God gave all of us pussies, but it's only a select few that are blessed with that good Power-U."

Frankie sucked her teeth. "Mo, you need to quit quoting them old ass Wu-Tang lines. I had the Method Man album too."

"Nah, I don't mean power-universal, I mean Power-U. That's when you're fucking a nigga so good that they ain't got no choice but to surrender all *power* to *you*."

"Your ass is warped, Mo," Frankie laughed.

"I wouldn't expect you to understand Frankie because you don't receive a regular dose of dick. When you got the good Power-U, all a nigga can say is '*ugh*,' or '*damn*' when he's sliding in and out. When the pussy is so warm that he gotta take his dick out just to make sure the condom hasn't accidentally slipped off. That, Frankie Five Fingers, is the good Power-U."

"And you, my best friend, are one theory short of the nut house," Frankie told her. "But seriously, I ain't trying to drive myself crazy over no nigga and his antics."

"Frankie you sound like a complete ass. You better not make that statement in front of nobody else but God. How is it all good when you're being faithful to this dude, and he's out doing him?"

"I didn't say he was doing him," Frankie corrected.

"You didn't have to say it, have you forgotten how long we've known each other? Look, I know that's your boo, but fuck Cowboy. Instead of chasing his thieving ass you need to go out and get you a *real* nigga."

"Mo, you know Cowboy is one of the realest niggaz on the streets. The whole hood knows what's up with him."

"Again, you're missing my point. Yeah, I know Cowboy is caked up and his gangsta is sho-nuff serious, but that don't make him a real nigga. A real nigga recognizes a good thing when he has it."

"Mo, Cowboy appreciates me. He just acts a fool sometimes."

"Sometimes? Baby, I ain't even gonna follow up with that one. More often than not that mutha fucka is showing his ass. Truth be told, I don't even know why you fuck with him like that."

"Because I love him," Frankie defended. There was conviction in her tone, but her eyes said different.

"Frankie, you don't love Cowboy, you love the idea of him. Every little girl wants to grow up and find the man that's gonna keep her fly and well fucked, but it goes deeper than that. I ain't gonna front like I wouldn't mind having a nigga like him, but at what cost, my happiness?"

"I am happy," she turned her head when she answered. When Mo turned Frankie back to face her, a lone tear rolled down her cheek.

"Bull shit," Mo said softly. "Frankie, I haven't seen you truly happy in five years and no matter how many niggaz you hook up with you can't get that back."

"Don't go there with me, Mo," Frankie jerked her head back. The sadness in her eyes was replaced by anger.

"I'd never, but I will say this. You can't spend the rest of your life chasing ghosts."

Frankie laughed. "I know, but what am I supposed to do when they start chasing me?"

# THIRTEEN

**The Doll House was jumping** more than usual on that cold December night. It was Friday, payday for the squares, and the fifteenth of the month, which was payday for the hustlers. Though Christmas wouldn't be there for at least another week and a half, people were getting into the spirit early. Strippers pranced around wearing next to nothing trying to get the patrons of the spot to part with their cash.

Against a wall, not far from where security guarded the door, two men posted up sipping cognac. The first of the two was about six-one and stocky. Though he was facing the stage where two girls were dancing, his eyes were on the bouncers. The second man was shorter, with skin the color of Mississippi Red Clay. A stocking cap covered his head, with neat cornrows tickling his shoulders. He kept shifting his weight from one leg to the other as if he couldn't decide which was more comfortable.

"You ready for this?" Cos asked, noticing that Duce kept fidgeting.

"Man, why do you keep asking me that when you know I am? You've seen how I get down, Cos," Duce reminded him.

"Yeah, I've seen it, but Cowboy and the others ain't convinced just yet. They're the ones you gotta prove yourself to, not me."

"Whatever," Duce said, sipping his drink. He had murdered a man for Cowboy and the bastard still wasn't convinced that he was a rider.

In an attempt to calm his nerves, Duce let his eyes wonder to the stage in the center of the room. A six-foot Spanish chick with thighs that looked like they could turn coal to diamonds strutted onto the stage. Her body was decorated in colorful tattoos, the most noteworthy of which was a magazine article she had been featured in. It covered her entire right ass cheek and part of her thigh.

She was dressed in a leather corset that pushed her huge breasts up, making them look like two melons that she tried to smuggle in her bra top. Jade green eyes stared out from beneath a mass of red hair, drinking in the onlookers. Her stiletto heels clicked on the wooden stage as she executed a cross-legged strut from one end to the other. The leather whip she carried cracked viciously on the ground ensuring she had every one's attention for her performance.

From the gym bag that sat on the edge of the stage, she produced a bottle of baby oil. She upturned the bottle letting the oil run down her neck and breasts. With slow, deliberate movements, she began massaging the oil into her skin, coating her in a slick glow. With oiled hands, she forced her double D breasts from the cups of the corset and began playing with the rings that were looped through her nipples. Never taking her eyes off the crowd, she gripped one of the rings between her teeth and began to tug at it. Cheers and whistles erupted from the horny men watching the show, followed by a shower of dollar bills.

She dropped down on all fours and started popping her ass to Rick Ross' *Hustling*. Ripples went through the soft flesh every time her ass made contact with the ground. With her ass cocked in the air, you could see the faint red hairs of her bush peeking out through the thong string. She reached back and began teasing the lips of her pussy with her index and middle fingers. Her face was somewhere between pain and pleasure as she dipped the two fingers inside her, jacked them in and out.

The stripper's thong, as well as the stage beneath her, were now soaked with baby oil and vaginal juices that seemed to trickle from her pussy like a slow leak. With a fluid motion, she yanked the thong off and tossed it into the crowd. A dude holding a Corona caught the thong and buried his face in it. Still toying with herself the stripper reached into the gym bag and pulled out a tube containing ping-pong balls. One by one, she licked the balls and began slipping them into her pussy. The crowd watched in amazement as the third ball disappeared into her vagina. The stripper flipped over on her back and spread her legs wide. Hiking her lower back off the ground with her hands, she began clapping her ass cheeks together in time with the beat. With a grunt, she began shooting the balls from her pussy into the air. By the time she had expelled the third ball, there was so much money on the stage that you could barely see the floor.

"Check it out," Cos said bringing Duce out of his wet dream. Duce followed his eyes to the other side of the room. A lone bouncer was standing against the wall next to a door marked PRIVATE. A man wearing a fur coat with a lady on each arm ambled over and greeted him. After exchanging a few words, the bouncer opened the door long enough to usher the man and his ladies through. In the few seconds that the door was open, they got a glimpse of the other section of the club. This was where the gambling went on.

"How much you think they're holding?" Duce asked, trying not to stare too hard.

"I don't know, but they won't be holding it for long," Cos ensured, pulling his jacket back exposing the small Uzi that hung from a shoulder sling.

A few seconds later, a girl came out of the back. She stood about 5'5" even though she was wearing high stiletto heels. The girl was dressed in a white bikini top with the matching thong. The flimsy string was almost invisible between her chunky sized ass cheeks. She leaned in and whispered something to Cos that Duce couldn't hear. Cos nodded and tucked a $100 dollar bill into her thong before sending her on her way.

"What was that all about?" Duce asked, not really understanding the exchange.

"A little advanced planning," Cos said and left it at that.

The two men continued to sip drinks and flirt with the strippers for about the next half hour or so. At several points, Duce found himself distracted by the pounds of flesh walking around the Doll House, but not Cos. He kept a constant vigil on the door making a mental note of everyone who entered or exited. Just when Duce was about to ask him when they were going to get it popping, he waved him silent and nodded towards the entrance of the club.

Thor's brutish form appeared in the doorway, with Cowboy on his heels. Both of their faces said 'strictly business.' Thor's broad back looked as if it would split the stitches on the three-quarter leather jacket he was wearing. When he moved, you could see the butt of his shotgun on one side, and what looked like a short mop handle on the other. The bouncers at the door spared Thor and Cowboy both a brief glance before turning away as if they hadn't seen them.

Cos made eye contact with Cowboy and nodded his head towards the door to the gambling spot. Keeping his hands low, he held down four fingers. Cowboy nodded and headed to the bar followed by his hulking friend. They sat at the bar just a few feet away from where the door to the gambling room was situated.

"Show time," Cos whispered in Duce's ear as he silently made his way across the room. Duce gave a brief look around and followed. Cos crept up slowly to where the door guard was standing and slid the small Uzi he was carrying from beneath his jacket. He took a minute to look around then pulled down the ski mask that had been rolled up on his head like a cap. Duce followed suit, pulling the stocking cap over his face.

When the guard turned around, Cos hit him with a sharp elbow to the gut. When the guard tried to double over Cos followed with a knee to the nose, breaking it. For the finishing touch, Cos whacked the guard in the back of the head with a small black jack, knocking him out. Before he could hit the ground, Duce caught him under the arm and placed him gently on a chair.

Duce had never heard him approach, but Thor was suddenly standing mere inches away from him. He gave the two men a checkered smile before pulling the ski mask down over his face. Reaching under his coat, opposite the shotgun, the man pulled out a very large sledge hammer. Swinging the hammer with all his might, Thor knocked the door to the gambling room off the hinges.

Big Sam Waters was a gambler, dope dealer and part-time pimp. Backed by some heavyweight cats from uptown, he had created the Doll House. It was a place where you could lose your money to one of the larcenous strippers who prowled it or in one of the dice games going on in the back. It was his pride and joy and because of it he was on his way to becoming a very rich man.

"How much is in here?" Moochie asked testing the

weight of the shopping bag he was carrying. He was a barrel chested man who sported a full beard and mustache. Notorious for his skills with a knife, and his willingness to use a gun, Big Sam had hired Moochie to make the money pick ups.

"Counting what we pulled in earlier this evening, about $40,000. There's another fifteen or so in the back, but I'm gonna keep that here just in case," Sam said, mauling a chicken leg. He was a large man with a big belly and lips that seemed to dominate most of his face.

"Sam, you need to stop keeping all this bread in here at one time. Arrange for three pickups instead of two."

"Fuck that, Mooch. This is a gambling spot. You gotta have enough bread in here to cover it if one of these mutha fuckas gets lucky. Never let it be said that Big Sam didn't pay his winners. Besides, that's why I got you making the pick ups. A nigga ain't stupid enough to go at you," he said, thinking of all the horror stories he had heard about Moochie. "Come on," Big Sam wiped his hands on a napkin and rose from behind his desk. His large gut bumped against the desk, almost spilling the two liter Diet Sprite he had been drinking. "I gotta hit the main floor to make sure these bitches are on their jobs." Big Sam and Moochie had made it out of the money room and halfway through the maze of gaming tables. when the door to the spot came crashing in.

The guard who had been standing behind the door caught the worst of it. The door, with the added weight of Thor's blow, knocked the guard to the ground, pinning him. With a grunt, Thor brought the sledge hammer high over his head and slammed it into the center of the fallen door. The man gurgled up blood and passed out, or died. No one checked to see which.

The second guard wouldn't be so easily taken. He drew his pistol and aimed it at Thor but Duce slapped his arm upward as soon as he pulled the trigger. Bullets ripped through the ceiling and rained plaster down on the gamblers. Duce followed with a sharp left to the head which succeeded in dazing the guard. Using every ounce of his strength, Duce hit the man with an uppercut to the chin, knocking him into the wall. The man tried to right himself to rush Duce but Cos stopped him by placing the barrel of the Uzi to his temple.

"Nigga, don't be stupid. Get yo ass on the floor!" Cos ordered. Not wanting to get shot, the guard did as he was told.

Moochie immediately went into action. Tossing Big Sam the bag containing the money, he drew his weapon and fired on the robbers. The high-powered slugs scattered people and money as Moochie tried to lay down anyone who wasn't on his team. Duce and Cos dove for cover, while Thor up-ended one of the tables and used it as a shield. Bullets splintered the wood and ripped through the cheap fabric Big Sam had used to cover them, but Moochie only managed to graze Thor's arm. The big man snarled and popped up from behind the table, letting off a quick burst from his shotgun. Moochie was able to get out of the way, but the same couldn't be said for a gambler who had poked his head up to try and lift some of the loose bills on the table. Stray pellets tore the side of his face off, sending him into a back spin.

The third guard, who had been watching from the other side of the room, cut loose with a Mac 10, hitting people and furniture. Duce executed a diving roll, narrowly escaping the bullets that tore into the wall where he had been standing only seconds prior. He moved with a fluidity that had been honed from years of stalking players of the underworld. He tumbled across the floor with his back coming to rest against a slot machine. For the moment he was safe, but the third guard kept firing, pinning him.

Cos dropped to one knee and squeezed the trigger of the Uzi, sweeping it upward. Bullets left a trail up the carpeted floor as well as the chest of the third guard. His body moved in a sick dance as Cos hit him from crotch to throat. Finally, he let up on the trigger long enough for the man to collapse onto the ground. Just as Cos was looking around to see how his partners were holding up, he heard shots coming from the next room.

The sounds of gunfire coming from inside the gambling spot were faint out in the club area, but Cowboy had been listening for them. When he was sure that his people had the party in full swing, he made his move. Putting on a pair of sunglasses, he drew a small machine gun from inside his jacket and climbed onto the bar. Firing the small submachine gun he aimed at the DJ booth. The turntables exploded bringing the music to an abrupt stop.

"You niggaz know what it is. Hands in the mutha fucking air and give up yo shit!" he ordered.

Hearing a shotgun blast, Cowboy's attention was temporarily drawn to the room at his rear. In the brief second he took his eyes off the crowd someone decided to play hero. The guy moved so fast that even if Cowboy had been looking in his direction he might not have been able to keep him from reaching his weapon. A small .38 was now pointed directly at Cowboy's chest. Before the hero could pull the trigger, his shoulder exploded.

A woman wearing a black wig and dark glasses was making military styled side steps across the club floor. In her hand she clutched two 9's. The guns jumped and expelled shells and she blew off different sections of the hero's body. The hero dropped to one knee and gurgled something just before she blew his brains onto the bar. The bartender belched and promptly threw up the Chinese food she had eaten before her shift.

"Any more heroes?" she asked, sweeping the crowd with her guns. No one moved.

"That's my boo, always right on time," Cowboy winked at her from behind his shades. "For a minute I thought you might've decided to sit this one out."

"Somebody has got to keep your arrogant ass from getting killed," she said, putting one more bullet into the dead man as she passed him. "How're the boys holding up?" she asked over her shoulder, careful not to take her eyes off the crowd. A second kick from the shotgun and a chunk of the wall being blown outward caused them both to duck.

"I'd say they've got it under control," Cowboy replied.

Moochie found himself trapped between Thor and Duce. He was returning fire as best he could, but knew that he was outgunned. Figuring a good run was a hell of a lot better than a bad stand, he began inching his way towards the rear door.

Duce was still crouched beside the slot machine gripping his Glock. The animal in him screamed for Moochie's blood, but he knew better than to make a target of himself out of anger. He had been killing for too long to make such a novice mistake. He needed an edge and an overturned bottle of Jack Daniels laying next him might've proven to be just that. Clutching the bottle about the neck, he tossed it in Moochie's direction. The bottle didn't come close to hitting Moochie head on, but Duce hadn't intended it to. When

Moochie's attention was drawn to the flying object, Duce let off two shots. When the bottle exploded, spraying Moochie with liquor and glass, the robbers were temporarily forgotten. This was the opening Duce had been waiting for. The first bullet hit Moochie high, shattering his collar bone and the second literally split his wig. Just as suddenly as it began, the fight was over.

Big Sam scurried along on all fours trying to put as much distance between himself and the blood bath as he could. The bag was clutched tightly against his chest. Covered in blood, he had to crawl through along the way. *Just a few more feet*, he thought to himself. He had made it all the way to the door, but when he reached up he didn't feel a door knob, but a belt buckle. Shakily, Big Sam looked up and found himself staring down the barrel of Cos' Uzi.

Cos backed out of the gambling room, with the shopping bag tucked under his arm and another looped around his wrist. If need be, he could fire the Uzi with one hand, but it wouldn't be as accurate. Thor and Duce covered his escape in case anyone else felt like they wanted to die. The gamblers they had just robbed were too scared to move let alone try something, but there was no need to take chances.

Duce moved on shaky legs almost slipping in a puddle of blood. His heart pumped so fast that he was lightheaded. Killing Marsha and Tic had been sweet, but not like this. It had been years since he had felt the rush of the kill and the junkie side of him wanted more of it. There was something about playing God with other people's lives that made his dick hard. Seeing Cowboy standing in the middle of the room giving orders brought a disgusted look to his face. Luckily, the stocking cap kept anyone else from seeing it.

He had expected Cowboy to be alone, but there was a female in the room with him. Something about the shape of her body and the way she moved was familiar to Duce, but he couldn't place her behind the disguise. She must've felt him staring at her because she turned around to face him. For a second, he thought he saw her body tense, but she quickly regained her composure.

"You got an eye problem?" she asked in a gruff voice.

"Nah," Duce turned away. Seeing her standing there holding two pistols both excited and frightened Duce.

"How was your first day on the job?" Cowboy asked.

Duce looked from the bodies in the gambling spot to the woman making her rounds and said, "Enlightening."

# FOURTEEN

**When they left the Doll House,** the five robbers split into two cars. Thor left with Cowboy and the familiar woman in the Navigator, while Duce rode in Cos' Honda with him. They were supposed to meet back at Cowboy's, but take two different routes to get there. Cowboy and his bunch hopped on the Major Deegan Expressway while Cos and Duce took the Cross Bronx. Cos fumbled with the radio leaving Duce to his thoughts.

"You did good, kid," Cos finally broke the silence. He coasted the Honda Accord at an even 60 miles per hour.

"Thanks," Duce said. "Ya man Cowboy knows how to plot."

Cos chuckled. "That's his M.O., master schemer. He puts the plans together and we execute with precision."

"So, I see. I'm just glad I didn't get my fucking head blown off in there."

"You handled yourself well in there, Duce. Like a true vet of this game."

"So, what was with the broad?" Duce asked innocently.

"Frankie? She's our wild card. That girl knows how to handle herself."

"Frankie?" *Impossible*, his brain screamed. Duce felt

all the color drain from his face. Of the millions of criminals in the city, why'd it have to be her? He tried to keep the expression on his face neutral, but Cos had already peeped him.

"Fuck is wrong with you, you know her or something?" Cos asked looking at Duce suspiciously.

"Nah, I just didn't expect another player in the game, especially a female," he lied.

Cos moved to the far left lane to pass a slow moving car. "Let me tell you something, Duce, I'm bull shit proof. I saw the way you were staring at Frankie and whatever you're thinking, un-think it."

"What're you talking about, Cos?" Duce asked.

"You know what I'm talking about. She's a sho-nuff fox, but off limits. She belongs to Cowboy."

"Is that right?" Duce asked sarcastically.

"Yeah, that's right. Duce, you're a good dude, but poking your nose around another man's woman is a sure way to get yourself killed."

"I was thinking the same thing," Duce mumbled.

Duce was silent for the rest of the ride, because he didn't trust his mouth not to betray his soul. Cos made small talk, but Duce only half listened. He occupied himself by looking at the passing scenery and tried not to think about Frankie. After about an hour of driving, they pulled the car over on 147th between Lenox and 7th in front of Espinard Gardens. Duce and Cos walked into the lobby of the building without a second glance from the security guard and boarded the elevator. They got off on the 8th floor and made their way to an apartment at the end of the hall. Before Cos even got a chance to ring the bell, Thor opened the door and waved them inside. The apartment was nice. Not too flashy or overly decorated, but just nice. There was a sofa, love seat and an entertainment system in the living room and four folding chairs, two of which were propped against the wall. Sitting on the love seat in front of the balcony was Cowboy. He had traded his black on black outfit for a pair of jeans and a t-shirt. On the table in front of him were stacks of money.

"Looks like we hit pay dirt," Cos said, taking a seat on the sofa. Duce didn't take the empty chair next to Thor, but leaned against the far wall watching Cowboy and the money.

"Nigga, we caked off. Between what we ripped off from the Doll House and what we got off the suckers in it, there's about 90 grand. That's over $18,000 a piece. Not bad for a few minutes work."

"Shit, I'll take jacking niggaz over a job any day," Thor said in his gravely voice. He was perched on one of the folding chairs with his hammer resting against his leg. The poor metal chair looked like it would give at any minute under the behemoth's weight.

"You and me both," Cos said, eyeing the money.

"Yo, kid," Cowboy turned to Duce. "You did good in there," he tossed him a bundle of money.

"I only did what you brought me in for," Duce said, fanning through the money before stuffing it into the inner pocket of his bubble coat.

"Spoken like a true G," Cowboy smiled. "Not for nothing, kid, that's small potatoes compared to the job we're gonna pull off on Christmas Eve. Them armored trucks are always lousy with cash."

"Bout how much you think we're gonna make off with, Cowboy?" Thor asked greedily.

"They'll be rounding up the bread from at least four check cashing spots, plus the stores in the shopping area that night. I'm guessing there'll be at least a half a mil or better."

"That's what the fuck I'm talking about!" Cos gave Thor a pound.

"Duce," Cowboy turned to him. "This was a test to see how you handled yourself, the next run will really determine if you're built like that, or if I'm kicking you the fuck outta my gang."

"Don't worry about me, son. When the time comes my hammer will ring the loudest," Duce said seriously.

"I told you my nigga was the real deal. Cowboy you should've seen this nigga on his Rambo shit inside the joint!" Cos said proudly.

"Why don't you say it a little louder, I don't think the neighbors heard you," Frankie said coming out of the bedroom.

She too had traded in her black on black outfit for something more becoming of her. She was now dressed in a tight fitting black sweater that drew attention to her ample breasts. She strutted across the room in a pair of gray wool slacks that hugged her ass and hips, but were cuffed at the bottom. Frankie had worn a wig and a wool hat for the robbery, but now her real hair was visible. It was a chocolate colored mane that she wore wrapped around her head with pins holding it in place. Her eyes lingered on Duce for a minute, but not long enough for anyone to catch the exchange her soul was making with his. For as much as she wanted to rush to him and embrace him, it would be a death sentence for both of them.

"Frankie Five, what da deal, ma?" Cos winked at her.

"Doing my part and then some," she replied.

"Yo, this is my boy Duce, the one Cowboy was telling you about," Cos introduced them.

"Nice to meet you," Frankie said, not looking at him. She didn't trust herself not to fall apart.

"Lighten up, baby, we nailed a big score," Cowboy pulled her down onto his lap. "We're gonna party our asses off!"

Frankie pushed herself up and looked at him, "After we come back, right?"

"Come back from where?" Cowboy asked, having no idea what she was talking about.

"Come on Cowboy, I know you didn't forget that I have to go to my brother's house in Mt. Vernon tonight so I can watch my niece in the morning? We were supposed to spend the night up there together."

"Tonight? Come on, baby we just pulled off a score. Don't you wanna enjoy the spoils for a while?"

"Cowboy, you know I can't shit on my brother like that. Unlike some of us I follow through when I say I'm gonna do something," she said with an edge to her voice.

"Frankie, you better watch your fucking mouth," Cowboy said in a deadly tone.

He didn't take kindly to her trying to style on him in front of his crew, and wasn't above slapping a female around to remind her of her place, but he knew with Frankie it would be an all out brawl.

Duce watched the exchange on edge. He hoped that Cowboy didn't get crazy, because if he did then he'd have to be put down sooner than expected, fucking up his whole plan. Thankfully he didn't.

"You know what, forget it," she stormed back into the bedroom, making a point to shoot Duce a nasty look as she went.

"Fucking females," Cowboy huffed.

"You better be careful, Cowboy. Frankie might fuck around and try to kill you in your sleep," Thor joked.

"That bitch is crazy, but she ain't stupid. I'm trying to party and she's on some old Adventures in Babysitting shit."

"You a cold dude, Cowboy," Cos teased him.

"Ice cold, my nigga!"

Cowboy got off the couch and walked over to the makeshift bar in the corner of the living room. He grabbed a bottle of Jack Daniels and filled four shot glasses. Moving back into the center of the living room, he handed each man a glass. "Yo, I wanna propose a toast. Here's to new blood in the family. Duce," he looked at the young man, "may your pockets be forever lined with cash and your hammer never jam."

The four men clinked glasses and downed the liquor.

Before the burning sensation from the drink had completely faded, Frankie came out of the bedroom. She was wearing an ankle length bubble coat and a wool hat with the brim flipped up on one side. Over her shoulder, she was carrying a gym bag. On her way out she kissed Cos and Thor on their cheeks, but shot Cowboy a scornful glare before slamming the door behind her.

"Well fuck you, too," Cowboy mumbled. "Well, since Frankie's ass is gone for the night I might as well call up some entertainment," he pulled out his cell phone.

"What we getting into, son?" Thor asked.

"*We*, is French, nigga. I'm gonna call that little freak bitch I met at the club last week."

"You mean the big butt hoe from 114th?"

"Yep," Cowboy said, grinning. "Shorty has been practically begging to come through here and suck me off."

"Ain't you worried about your girl doubling back and catching you?" Duce asked, hoping that he sounded more concerned than mocking.

"Nah, she's pissed at me so it'll be at least a day or two before I see her again. Besides, if she do come back and find my dick jammed in this bitch's throat she can either join in or wait her turn," Cowboy said like he was the man.

"You need to stop hoarding the pussy and share," Cos joked.

"And what you need to do is get yourself some game so you can get your own bitches. Cowboy is a one man show. Now, y'all niggaz get the fuck outta my pad so I can handle my business."

Everyone laughed except Duce. Though he and Cowboy didn't know each other very well, he couldn't stand the man. He was loud, arrogant and sneaky. If it had been up to him, he would've just popped him and been done with it, but he knew he couldn't carry it like that. If he made a move against Cowboy he'd have to move on the whole crew. If it came down to it, he wouldn't lose any sleep over killing Thor, but Cos was his man. And when he did get at Cowboy what would Frankie do? Would she seek revenge for her murdered lover or would she thank Duce for freeing her?

# FIFTEEN

**When Duce, Cos and Thor got outside,** it had started snowing again. The temperature had dropped but it was nowhere near as cold as it could've been for December. Cos and Thor got in the Honda while Duce walked down Lenox to where his Eddie Bauer was parked. He had his hands tucked deep into the pockets of his coat, fingering his pistol. There was something about committing mass murder that put him on edge.

It was a short walk to 141$^{st}$ street where his truck was parked, but the slick snow made it a pain in the ass. He bleeped his alarm and jumped behind the wheel, glad to be out of the element. Duce put his key in the ignition and the truck roared to life. He had just put the truck in drive when he felt something cold against the back of his neck. He glanced up at the rear view mirror and could see Frankie's fierce brown eyes staring back at him. When he opened his mouth, she pressed the gun deeper into his neck.

"Shut the fuck up and drive," she hissed. Duce nodded and pulled into traffic.

Cos and Thor cruised through the silent night in the

Honda. The sounds of The Isley Brother's *Between the Sheets* played softly through speakers, while Cos hummed along. He was a stickler for the oldies. Thor sat beside him bobbing his head. He was more into rap music but like with most savage beasts, the music soothed him. He was squirming in the passenger seat trying to get comfortable. Even though he had the seat pushed back as far as it would go, his legs still felt cramped. He cursed under his breath, wishing for the hundredth time that he hadn't left his truck at home.

"Cos, when are you gonna get rid of this tiny ass car?" Thor asked.

"When you buy me another one," Cos shot back. "I've had this car for years and it's always held me down. It's a good ride."

"Yeah, if you're a fucking circus midget," Thor teased him. "Say, what you think about Duce?" he changed the subject.

"I think the young boy handled himself pretty well for it to be his first job," Cos said.

"That's just it. He handled himself a little *too* well."

Cos cut his eyes at the big man. "Why are you so fucking paranoid?"

"You can never be too careful, Cos. Look at what happened to Ace." Ace was a dude that they both knew from around the neighborhood. He was getting money on the streets until he gave his cousin a job. Six months later when the Feds rushed his spot, he discovered that his cousin had been a Confidential Informant.

"Thor, you're bugging. Duce ain't no rat."

"I ain't saying he's a rat Cos, but there's more to that kid than he's telling. He gunned that dude down without batting an eye."

"Well, he was locked up for a body so I know he ain't no stranger to murder," Cos informed him.

"Speaking of which, did he ever tell you what went down with that? How the fuck does a nigga go down for a body and come home in five?"

"I felt a little funny about it too, so I had him checked out. His government name is Melvin Bernard."

"Bernard," Thor scratched his head trying to figure why he felt a chill at hearing the name. "Why does that name sound so familiar?"

"Maybe you fucked his girl," Cos joked. "From what I read in his jacket, he blew trial on a double murder and the judge gave him the long walk. A lot of niggaz scream that they're innocent in the pen, but there was something in his eyes that almost made me believe him. Son fired his trial lawyer and handed over every penny he had to that slick talking Israeli cat who got that rapping nigga outta that rape shit. The odds of him getting the conviction overturned was so slim that I made him show me the original copies of his paperwork before I even agreed to talk any business with him. It reads just like he's giving it up, he's good."

"Well, I ain't so sure and I'm gonna keep my eyes on that sneaky mutha fucka."

"Thor, let that boy alone. He saved our asses in there; I think he's proven himself."

"Not to me, Costello. The average mutha fucka just moves off survival instinct in a gunfight, but home boy was on some real Matrix shit, so that means he's a pro and if he's a pro then why haven't we ever heard of him? I'm telling you, this shit is like trying to stuff triangles into squared holes."

"Whatever, nigga," Cos waved him off. "You need to get your mind off Duce and on this heist we're gonna pull on Christmas Eve. This will be our biggest score ever!"

"You think there's gonna be as much cake as Cowboy says?" Thor asked.

"More than likely. Cowboy does his homework on regular jobs, so I know he's checked this front, back and sideways. Even if it's close to a half mil, we'll be straight for a while. Say, what're you gonna do with your portion of the money?"

"Buy your ass a bigger car!" Thor laughed.

Frankie directed him down Lenox Avenue to 132$^{nd}$ where he made a left. They continued another three blocks until they reached Park Avenue and hung a right. Frankie told Duce to pull the truck under the L and kill the engine. For a long while there was complete silence. Duce thought about saying something, but the fact that she still had the gun pressed against his neck deterred him. Finally, Frankie moved back and allowed him to let go of the breath that he hadn't even realized he was holding.

"Give me one good reason why I shouldn't smoke yo creep ass," Frankie hissed. Her voice was cold, far colder than he remembered.

"Frankie, if you'd just put the gun down we could talk about this."

"Talk," she cocked the hammer back with her thumb. "I ain't heard a fucking word from you in five years and now you wanna communicate? Nigga, you gotta come better than that."

"It ain't what it looks like," he said, trying to remain as still as possible. Ninety eight percent of the time a woman scorned plus a gun equaled a dead man and he had no interest in becoming a statistic.

"Derrick, let's not even talk about what it looks like, because if my mind and my heart take me there, as sure as my ass is black you're a dead man," she said seriously. "How and what the fuck are you doing here?"

"You want me to answer the questions in that order, or just wing it?" he said, trying to be cute.

"I'm the one with the gun, so I'm asking the questions," she reminded him.

"Looks like we've got ourselves a Mexican stand off," he motioned downward. Frankie hadn't noticed it, but Duce had managed to slip his gun from his pocket at some point and had it pointed at her lower body.

"Sneaky son of a bitch," she said, tucking her pistol back into her overnight bag.

"If that isn't the pot," he put his gun away. "Since when did you start running around with low life mutha fuckas like Cowboy?"

"Since my *so called* man disappeared on me five years ago!" she shot back.

"That was a low blow," he said softly.

"Low blow, for a low mutha fucka. Duce you've got some nerve. You leave me high and dry to pop up years later pulling capers with my man and I'm supposed to welcome you with open arms?"

Duce pinched the bridge of his nose. "Frankie, it wasn't like that."

"Then what was it like, Duce? You drop me off one night and the next morning you're on the news!"

"Frankie, I got blindsided. You think I had a choice in what happened to me? Fuck no!" He hadn't meant to be so sharp, but the card was already laid. "Ma, I know I should've got word to you, but…"

"But what, nigga? Duce, do you have any idea what you put me through? What am I supposed to think when all my visits are denied and my letters go unanswered. And the one time your monkey ass does have the common decency to respond, it's to kick some old funny-style shit about how you're dead to me. What the fuck was that, Derrick?"

Duce found himself at a loss for words. From the moment the police rolled into the apartment, he knew he was finished. Frankie had been his heart since before he even knew what to do with a girl, so whether she would ride the bid with him or not wasn't a question, but he couldn't condemn her to that. He loved Frankie too much to sentence her to life as a prison wife, so he reluctantly let her go.

"Frankie," Duce sighed, "letting you go was the hardest thing I've ever had to do in my short life, and please believe that it's a decision that has haunted me throughout my whole bid, but you gotta understand where my head was at. These crackers had me by the balls and the only promise of freedom made to me was to be carried out in a pine box. Seventeen," his eyes took on a far off look. "That's how many times I thought about killing myself because I knew I'd never see you again. I could never bring myself to ask you to ride that bid with me Frankie. I did it to protect you."

Frankie looked at Duce as if he had lost his mind. "Protect me? Since when did I become the damn damsel in distress? Duce you and Knowledge tore them streets up, but don't forget that we came up in this thing together, so I ain't no virgin to pain or bloodshed. This is Frankie Five Fingers," she pounded her chest. "While you were bull shitting, how many of those messes did I help you clean up?"

He wanted to protest but he knew she was right. Frankie went above and beyond for her man. From helping tend his wounds to lying to the police, Frankie held him down. She was the rib Adam had sacrificed to create Eve.

"That's just it, Frankie. I had pulled you in deep enough and I couldn't drag you down any further. You're my heart, Frankie Five Fingers," he said emotionally.

Frankie felt herself about to cry, but wouldn't. She had already shed a thousand and one tears for Duce and didn't have any left. "You could've said something, Duce. I was your gangsta bitch, ride or die for my nigga, remember that?" she reminded him of their oath.

Duce nodded. "So now you're riding or dying for Cowboy?" he asked sarcastically.

Without warning Frankie reached around and slapped fire out of Duce. Frankie attacked him with the fury of a caged animal, drawing blood from his lip. Duce managed to crawl up on his knees and grab Frankie about her wrists. He tried to push her down in the seat but she reversed the move and pulled him into the back seat with her. Frankie bit into Duce's shoulder like a dog on a bone. He slammed her against the seat hard enough to knock the wind out of the average chick, but Frankie kept coming.

He'd finally managed to pin her arms and it was around that time when their eyes met and time stood still. Their lips met in a mess of skin and teeth. It wasn't the kiss of reunited lovers, but rapist and victim. Frankie gnawed at his tongue while Duce tried to suck the breath from her lungs. Frankie dug a pocket knife from her bra and softly down the length of his torso, cutting it open in a perfect line. When her tongue touched the crease in his chest, Duce shuddered.

With just touch, Frankie sent shockwaves through Duce's body. She licked and nibbled on his nipples until they were almost as hard as his cock. When she looked up at him with those fierce brown eyes, he didn't see malice or resentment, only hunger. The same hunger that ravaged his insides.

In a deft motion, he had her shirt over her head and was tossing it in the front seat before she even realized he'd moved. Slipping the hands under her bra cups, he massaged each one of her breasts and lost himself in the softness of her skin.

Everywhere Duce touched her left a warm sensation. She remembered the touch well and had craved it ever since he'd left her. Her eyes traveled down the length of his chest and came to rest on his crotch. Her hands shook so bad that she almost couldn't get the throbbing muscle out of the jeans. She tested the weight of his penis in her hand and smiled, watching it bob up and down with his breathing.

Duce braced his arms between the headrest of the driver's seat and the cushion of the back seat. He tried to maintain his cool, but when he felt her warm mouth on his dick he melted. She slowly licked the shaft from the balls up and wrapped her lips around the head. Frankie took him into her mouth a little at a time at first but as they got into a rhythm, she opened her throat and let him push deep enough to gag her. Frankie's lips on him felt so good that twice he thought he was going to faint. He ran his hands through her silken hair dislodging the pins as he went. Frankie looked exotic staring at him from behind the veil of hair making him even crazier.

Feeling himself about to nut, he pried her hungry mouth loose and pulled her to him for a kiss. His clumsy hands popped the buttons off her jeans in his rush to get them off, and she wiggled a leg out. Duce propped her leg on his shoulder and shoved his face into her crotch. The sweet smell of lilac and Dove soap was intoxicating. His middle finger looked as if it might've been dipped in cake batter when he dipped it in and out of her. He sucked her juices off his fingers and pressed his lips to hers so that she could share the nectar. When their bodies could no longer be denied, their souls were reunited.

Even with her being wet, he had to shove himself into her, causing her to cry out. He tried to pull away but she gripped his ass cheeks forcing him deeper. Frankie's nails raked down Duce's back as he plowed her causing him to pump faster. Caught in the most perfect moment of his life, Duce had no idea how long they'd been going at it, but he could feel the eruption building in his cock. Frankie must've felt it too because she locked her legs around his waist and wouldn't let him pull away. Duce howled like a wounded coyote when he came, but you couldn't hear it over Frankie's own shriek of pleasure. Cum ran from her pussy, down his thighs and onto the seats of his truck. He didn't care though. All that mattered was that he had been reunited with the love of his life, his gangsta bitch.

# SIXTEEN

**Duce and Frankie lay huddled** in the back seat of the Eddie Bauer watching the sunrise over the East River. The hazy clouds floating across the orange sky bore a striking resemblance to sherbet ice cream. Frankie's brother was going to be pissed for her standing him up, but he had to understand; miracles only came along once in a lifetime.

The reunited lovers had enjoyed each other until neither could go anymore, but they still gave it one more shot before giving up. Duce's nuts felt like someone had squeezed every once of fluid from them and Frankie's insides were sore but they both reasoned that it had been well worth it. For the last five years, the both of them had been two wondering halves, but now they were whole.

"My brother is gonna kill me," Frankie said, tracing the line of Duce's chest with her finger.

"Your brother, shit, I'd thought you'd be more worried about Cowboy finding out what we did," he said smugly.

Frankie sat up and looked at him. "Well, it wouldn't have been any of Cowboy's business if you'd kept it gangsta with me. You can start if you want to Derrick, but believe I'll finish it."

Duce matched her tone. "What? You getting mad because I'm kicking some real shit? You belong to that lame ass nigga now."

"First of all, mutha fucka, I don't belong to nobody. Frankie Five is and has always been her own woman, whether it was in your bed or Cowboy's," she pulled her purse closer to her. "Now you've got one more time to try and insinuate I'm some whore bitch and we're gonna have an issue, you understand?"

"Frankie, go ahead with that extra shit," he told her, but didn't take his eyes off her bag. He was seeing a whole new side of Frankie and wasn't sure if he was prepared to deal with it. "Ain't nobody trying to call you out your name or nothing, I'm just telling you what it is. You don't think Cowboy would wild out if he found out that I fucked his broad?"

"So, that's what this is all about? You had sex with me to get under Cowboy's skin?" Frankie snatched her pants off the floor and began sliding them on, completely forgetting about her underwear.

"Hold on," he grabbed her arm. "Frankie, I was and *still* am, madly in love with you. This had nothing to do with getting under Cowboy's skin. I've got something way nastier planned for that mutha fucka."

Frankie looked at him confused. "I don't get it. One minute you guys are smiling and shooting shit up together and the next you act like he kicked your dog or something. What's the deal with you and Cowboy?"

"Ain't no deal, I'm just trying to get back on my feet," he lied.

Frankie twisted her lips. "Duce, miss me with all that. Even after the lawyer fees you left me with almost a hundred stacks, and if I had a hundred then you had quadruple that tucked away, so I know you ain't hard up for paper. We've never lied to each other in the past, so let's not start now."

Duce pondered lying, but she knew him too well not to

see through it. "Frankie," he began, "you know I love you, right?"

"Duce, please just spit it out."

"I joined Cowboy's team to kill him," he said flatly. If Duce noticed the shock that flashed in Frankie's eyes, he made no mention of it.

"Kill him, why?" she asked.

"Frankie, who do you think set me up?"

Frankie was confused at first, but then her eyes flashed recognition. "Cowboy put the murders on you?" she asked in shock.

"Not personally but that pussy gave the order. My brother was the man, and all these mutha fuckas was jealous of him. There wasn't a nigga on the block who didn't want to be my brother, but all knew that to take his spot you had to go through his shadow," Duce pounded his chest. "My brother was a great and fair business man, but his heart wasn't cold enough," Duce said emotionally. "He wasn't like me…he wasn't a killer."

"Duce…" she began.

"Let me finish," he placed a finger gently over her lips. "All I ever thought about was murdering the men who crossed my brother. I needed a way to cut into this Cowboy nigga, and my ticket came through when I met an inmate named Costello Brown who was coming through on a robbery beef." He went on to explain to Frankie how he'd met Cos in prison and they'd become fast friends. "Once I plugged in to him, murdering his man would've been a cake walk, but I was still sitting on life and waiting on an appeal. You know I ain't never been real religious, but I got down on my knees and did some serious praying. I know it's wrong, but I promised the powers that be if I got out of prison I was gonna balance the scales. Now, I don't know if it was God or the Devil, but a few years later my prayers were answered."

Frankie eyed him suspiciously. "Cowboy is a cunning and cautious man. How in the world did you get him to accept you as a part of the crew with him knowing he'd not only killed your brother, but sent you to jail in the process?"

"Because the arrogant son of a bitch never made the connection. Frankie, the only people that called me Duce were you, Granny and Knowledge. Everybody on the street knew me as D or Derrick, if they were from the old neighborhood. D-Murder was a phantom, and I was locked up under the name Melvin Bernard. The bulls fucked up and listed my middle name first, but it ended up working to my advantage when me and Cos got tight. D-Murder was the muscle behind the Uptown Boys, and Melvin was some poor lump sitting on life."

Frankie's head was spinning at what Duce was revealing to her. She'd known that Cowboy could be ruthless, but until that moment she hadn't realized how much so. There were a thousand questions running through her head, but there was one she had to know the answer to.

"How?"

He knew what she was asking without her having to say. "Your boys provided me with that. One night Cos was bragging to me about this homicide cop that his man Cowboy had on the payroll who let him and Thor kill recklessly. As soon as he slipped and said the name I recognized it from my case. It was the same cock-sucker that arrested me at the murder scene. I put damn near every dime I had on the streets and then I had my people make two phone calls; the first was to inform some suspicious cats at Internal Affairs that this pig had a key of blow in his trunk, and the second was to make sure it was there when they caught up with him. I ain't gonna give you all the details, baby, but just know that price I had to pay for my freedom isn't something I'd be willing to negotiate again."

"Damn, Duce, that's some heavy shit."

"Heavy is an understatement love, but I thank them old heads everyday for always telling me about keeping a low profile. My brother loved the spotlight and I was glad for him to have it, but all I cared about was the paper. If my paper wasn't straight then I was coming for your head. You remember those days, ma."

Frankie rubbed her arms as if a wind had appeared from nowhere. "Yeah," she said, just above a whisper. Her mind drew up old images of Duce creeping in with blood splattered on his boots.

Duce chuckled. It wasn't the normal charismatic laugh that Frankie had known, but something darker. She couldn't imagine what Duce must have been feeling all those years as she had never been in that position, but she could feel it seeping from him like sweat on a summer day. She wanted to reach out and touch his face, but there was something about the set of his jaw that made her hesitate.

"Cowboy is the loose end," he continued after a long pause. "That snake took five years of my life, my brother and apparently my girl," he half-joked. Tears welled in his eyes but never fell. "So you see Cowboy has to die."

"I had no idea," Frankie sobbed.

"I know," he stroked her cheek. "When I came back here to take my revenge I never imagined that fate would further mock me by having you share Cowboy's bed." Frankie tried to turn away but Duce wouldn't let her. "There's no shame in that Frankie. I was gone and I guess you needed someone to turn to. I ain't mad at you boo. The question is, now what? Do you run and tell your lover what I plan to do, or do you turn the other cheek while I lullaby his ass?"

"Duce, you know I'd never betray you, no matter how I feel about the situation."

"Then fall back and let me boogie."

"Damn, you and your vengeful ass nature," she placed her head in her hands. The thought of losing Duce again made her feel ill. "Why can't you just let it go? We can go away together and start fresh," she pleaded.

"Baby girl if it were only that simple. Cowboy took everything I ever loved and now he's going to pay. I'm gonna take his life and his money, the same way he did my brother."

Frankie laughed. It was all she could do to keep from falling down and crying. "Cos and Thor aren't gonna stand by and let you get at Cowboy. Even if you do manage to kill him, they'll hunt you down."

"I wouldn't too much worry about that. I've put something together to get them out of the way while I handle their boss."

"There'll be others, Duce. Cowboy knows a lot of people."

"Like I give a shit. By the time it all hits the fan I'll be on my way to the Dominican Republic. I got a little piece of land down there that I can sit on for a few," he informed her.

This took Frankie by surprise. She couldn't help but to wonder if he acquired the land while he was away, or while he was with her but neglected to say anything. "You've got it all mapped out, huh?"

"Just about, all I need to know now is where you stand?"

"Duce, I told you I'd never betray you."

"Oh, I don't doubt that, but Cowboy is your man. I'd be a fool to think you could just watch him die and not feel any way about it. I'd love to have you at my side when this is all over, but if not I'll understand. I'm not trying to …"

Frankie placed a finger over Duce's lips, quieting him. "Duce, I've been in love with you since we were ten years old, no matter what you did or how long you were gone, that hasn't changed."

"So, you're my gangsta bitch again?" he asked, with glassy eyes.

"Silly boy, I never stopped being your gangsta bitch. Your enemies are my enemies, ride or die baby."

Looking into Frankie's eyes, he wondered how he could've been foolish enough to let her go in the first place. Chicks like her were only supposed to come along once in a lifetime and he had been twice blessed. It was a blessing that he had no intentions on squandering again. He took Frankie in his arms and kissed her as if it would be the last time.

"What was that for?" she asked, slightly out of breath.

"For not holding my foolish pride against me," he said.

"Oh, don't get it fucked up. I have every intention on letting you make it up to me, but we can talk about that later. Now, Cowboy won't be easy to kill, so I know you've got a plan?"

He smirked. "Don't I always? Let me run it down to you, boo."

# SEVENTEEN

**Duce found the burdens of his** vow suddenly weighing very heavy on him. When he had pieced his plan together, he'd gone through every possible outcome, or so he'd thought. Running into Frankie hadn't been part of the equation. He had intended to look her up after his business with Cowboy was concluded but discovering she was a member of his crew as well as his lover added an unexpected twist.

Just thinking about them together made Duce mad as hell. He couldn't shake the images flashing through his mind of them being together. *Did she do the things to Cowboy that she used to do to him?*, Duce wondered. Another thing that Duce had been trying not to think of was how far could he trust Frankie? They had been lovers once, but five years is a long time to be away and time tends to change people. What if she had taken his plan to Cowboy and they were laying a trap for him. Without the element of surprise, his chances of killing Cowboy were slim to nil. He could see them now laughing together over his ruined corpse.

Duce took a deep breath and tried to clear his head of the images. Back in the days, he and Frankie had banged out side by side, but now she was standing on the other side of the fence which could complicate things considerably. He might be too focused on Frankie to handle his business with

Cowboy. Duce was a seasoned killer, but men like Cowboy were not to be taken lightly. Still, his brother's killers had to be dealt with, and if he had to go through Frankie to get it done then so be it.

The constant, falling snow had made navigating through the large cemetery quite the task. He had to trek across the grass to keep from busting his ass on the icy cobble stones. A few yards ahead of him he could see the top of the tombstone. Even if he hadn't gotten directions from the ground's keeper, he would've been able to find the grave. The headstone was made from black marble and stood easily four feet off the ground. Perched atop the stone was a sculpted angel with its arms stretched to the heavens. Duce had commissioned the design from a talented young prison artist, and Reggie did the leg work on the streets to get it done. It was a parting gift to Knowledge.

Duce knelt on the snow-covered grass, soaking his jeans and sending a chill through his knees. He ignored the biting cold as he wiped the clumps of snow from the headstone. The words 'God's Favorite' were engraved into the marble, just above his brother's name, birth and death dates. It had been five years since his brother had been murdered, but it seemed like just yesterday they were getting high and cracking jokes. Those were the good times and in the blink of an eye, Cowboy had ensured that there would be no more.

"What da deal, son?" Duce said to the grave. "I know you're probably pissed that it took me five years to visit you but, incase you haven't heard, I've been indisposed," Duce chuckled. "Man, this shit feels weird, me talking to you like this. I always thought that it would be the other way around with someone laying me down. I guess the good really do die young. I ain't gonna get all emotional on you cause that's not how we do, but a nigga miss you, big bro." Only when Duce felt something warm splash onto his hand did he realize that he was crying.

"Look at me, out here bawling like a damn baby. I guess being overly emotional is just one more of my short-comings. Don't even trip though, cause them niggaz that brought all this shit down on us are history. That snake bitch Marsha is outta here and that bitch ass nigga Scott. I'm knocking Butch out the box this morning. I'll bet his ass ain't expecting what I got for him when he wakes up all happy and shit this morning," Duce laughed. "The last piece of the puzzle is Cowboy. I've got a nice Christmas present for him." Duce got up from the grave and brushed his knees off. "Big brother, it's gonna be a while, if ever, before I can come back and visit you. You know I gotta fly the coop after I push these niggas' shit back. I ain't trying to stick around for the fall out. But you know what, I don't need to come all the way out here to talk with you…because I'll always have you in my heart," he pounded his chest. "Take care of yourself my nigga, and hold a place for me up there," he looked to the sky. Duce lowered his head and walked away.

With each step he took in the soft snow, his hate for Cowboy intensified. He had failed his brother once, but it wouldn't happen again. He would either kill Cowboy or die trying.

"What it is brother? I know you gotta task for me today. I'm trying to get a bottle and I'm two dollars short?" old man Jim capped as Butch stepped into the barbershop. Jim was an old wine head who did odd jobs for everybody in the neighborhood. He was a pain in the ass, but he was al-ways willing to work for his pennies.

Butch gave him a toothy grin. "Jim, since today is such a special day, I'm gonna lay a $20 on you for five minutes of your time."

"Talk about it, boss," Jim rubbed his hands together.

Butch dug in his pocket and handed Jim a crisp $50 dollar bill. "I want you to run up the street and grab me a dozen roses."

"Aw shit, let me find out you got a new tender you about to break in. Is she sweet, boss?"

"I wouldn't know, mutha fucka. The flowers are for my daughter. She's auditioning at LaGuardia today."

"My bad Butch, you know I didn't mean no disrespect to ya, brother," Jim shrank a bit. "Wow, little Penny was always good on them keys, I hope she makes it!" Jim said over his shoulder as he shuffled down the street.

Butch's baby brother, Harvey, stood a few feet away, eyes nervously scanning the street. He'd have been more comfortable cooking and cutting drugs than playing Butch's bodyguard for the morning, but it was a last minute decision. Butch's wife, Liz, was adamant about him not bringing his usual goon squad to their daughter's audition, as not to give off the wrong idea. After what had gone down with young Scotty, there was no way Butch was rolling to the event alone. Harvey was a chicken shit, but even he should be able to handle the security detail at a little girl's recital for a few hours.

He'd gotten the wire about Scotty getting smoked, couldn't say he was surprised. Scotty had been abusing and burning people left and right since Butch put him in pocket. He'd warned him time and again to slow down, but Scotty did what he pleased. They said that he got laid near Willie's which disappointed Butch further. He'd stressed to Scotty the importance of not developing a routine, and the fact that he was now dead was just the reason why.

"What's popping, Jessie," Butch lowered himself into the first chair. "I ain't got time for the whole cut, just give me a shave and a line up so I can make a move. I got a special appointment, so I need you to make my line extra sharp, feel me?"

"You know how I do it," Jessie assured him, draping the smock around his neck. "So, your little girl's got something going on?" he asked, using a brush to whip the shaving cream in a small bowl. Most barbers did their shaves with clippers, but Jessie was old school.

"Yeah man, they're giving her a second chance to audition. She won't be able to attend until next year, when she's a sophomore, but I could give a damn so long as she gets in. That's one hell of a school," Butch settled back in the chair.

"I know what you mean, man. LaGuardia is supposed to be one of the best for music and art," Jessie began applying the shaving cream to Butch's face and neck.

Butch closed his eyes and spoke through slightly parted lips. "And that's why I'm pushing so hard to get her in there. My baby is smart and talented as hell, but you can never have too many edges when those colleges call."

"So, you think the colleges pick solely based on what high school them kids came out?" Jessie began dragging the razor smoothly across Butch's face.

"I know it to be true, Jessie. You take a regular kid from let's say, high school A and compare it against a kid from LaGuardia. The kid from high school A might have better grades, but the kid from LaGuardia comes from better credentials, so he stands a better chance. Most times it ain't what you know…it's who you're with."

"You sure as shit ain't lying about that," Jessie chuckled. Butch's eyes were still closed so he couldn't see the slack look that had come over Jessie's face. He'd never heard the door open, or the foot steps when the man crossed the short distance between the bar and the first chair and pressed a pistol against Jessie's neck. Jessie, careful not to move a muscle, looked to the right and found himself staring into a pair of dead eyes. Slumped in one of the folding chairs was Harvey. He had one hand halfway to his gun and his neck was bent at a funny angle. Upon closer inspection, Jessie noticed the Timberland string tied around his neck. The poor bastard never stood a chance. The young man raised his hands to his lips and motioned for silence as he plucked the razor from Jessie's trembling hand and nodded for him to back away. Seeing what he was capable of, Jessie did the wise thing and complied.

"Yeah, Jessie, I got big plans for that girl," Butch continued. "I spent years on the block getting it up so that my little girl wouldn't have to want for anything. She ain't gonna be no lump on the street like we were, trying to get by on our wits."

"Because wits don't always prevail," Duce whispered into Butch's ear. Butch's eyes popped open and when he saw the man sneering at him in the mirror, he almost shit his pants. If it weren't for the razor pressed into his jugular, he would have surely fainted.

Duce slid the razor up a bit, but didn't apply enough pressure to draw blood. "Come on, Butchy. You don't remember my name no more?"

"D…D-Murder," Butch trembled just getting the name out.

"So, the liar has found its tongue," Duce tapped Butch on his shoulder with the barrel of his gun. "I hear you're doing big things in the world, Butch. You got that pot money? *'No matter what we make, ten percent goes in the pot for the family so every nigga on our team can have lawyer money or be buried properly'*. Remember that, son?"

"Derrick, what's this shit all about, man?" Butch tried to add some bass to his voice, but it kept cracking.

"Oh, I think you know what it's all about, fam. My brother rests with the lord and you're out here rubbing shoulders with his murderers. How do you think that shit was looking to the brothers on the tier? Let me answer that for you," he moved the blade so quickly that Butch didn't feel the stinging until Duce was standing in front of him. "It sounds like you're a cock sucking piece of shit that would sell his mother down the drain for a street corner."

"Nigga is you crazy?" Butch clasped his neck. He tried to hop out of the chair, but Duce kicked him back down.

"Nah, I ain't crazy brother," Duce slashed him across his protruding gut. "Just vindictive. Take your medicine with pride," Duce advanced on Butch with the razor, but Butch rolled out of the chair and landed on all fours.

"You're making a mistake," Butch pleaded from his knees, damn near groveling.

"I'm not making a mistake," Duce snatched Butch roughly to his feet by his jowls. "I'm correcting one," he drew back for the killing blow, but Butch had a parting question.

"Wait…I can't go out like this, what about my little girl!"

Duce hesitated as if he were about to change his mind before a chill crept into his eyes. "Shit, what about her?" he asked before opening Butch up. The man flapped around on the floor like a wounded fish for almost five minutes before he finally lost the battle. Duce turned to the old barber and leveled his pistol.

Jessie backed up with his hands held high. "Come on, Derrick, don't do me like this. I've been cutting you and your brother's heads since back when you were little boys, you know me, man."

Duce nodded in satisfaction and lowered his gun. "Yeah, I know you Mr. Jessie, so I know you gonna keep your mouth shut about what happened here, right?"

"I did ten years in the joint and ain't never let any nigga's name but mine roll off my tongue," Jessie said proudly.

Duce reached into his pocket and handed Jessie a wad of bills. The old barber was too scared to count it. "Sorry about the mess I made," Duce headed for the door. As an afterthought he added, "Does your daughter still live down on ninety-something street in those projects?" Jessie's dark skull suddenly became very pale. He thought he might be suffering a mild heart attack until Duce gave him that little boy smile. "I'm just playing with you, Mr. Jessie." And just like that,

D-Murder was gone.

# EIGHTEEN

**Frankie moved as silently as the grave** through the streets of Bed-Stuy, Brooklyn. Night had fallen hours ago and there wasn't much of anyone on the streets other than the dealers and stick-up kids. Frankie wasn't worried about the latter because she was armed with a Desert Eagle. Even if it weren't for the large pistol, the trained eye could see the shadow of death looming over her like a protective shield.

She was dressed in black jeans and a skully, with a black Woolrich coat that almost swallowed her. The soft, but filthy, snow crunched under her feet as she walked. The hood of her coat was pulled halfway around her head, enough so that she could fight off some of the chill, but not too much as to obscure her vision. Frankie wasn't one to be caught slipping.

Frankie passed a group of young men who were loitering in front of the bodega on Throop and Hancock. One of them said something to her as she passed, but she ignored the comment and kept her stride. Not having anything better to do, the boys fell in step behind her. They whistled and made cat calls, but Frankie didn't respond. She wanted to turn around and slap fire out of the boys, but didn't. She was trying to keep a low profile and getting into a fist fight in the middle of the street might draw unwanted attention to her.

Cowboy had eyes everywhere.

Tiring of the cat and mouse game, one of the boys pressed his luck and grabbed Frankie by the arm. Spinning, she clocked him with a left to the side of the head and followed with a right to the jaw, knocking him down but not out. The boy snarled and struggled to his feet but before he could reach Frankie, she had drawn her weapon and was pointing it at his head.

"You got frog in you?" she asked, pulling the slide back on the gun with her free hand. "Go ahead, I dare you."

"We don't want no problems, miss," one of the boys said.

"Oh, ain't no fun fighting a girl that might fight back, huh?" she mocked, sweeping the gun over all of them. "You niggaz beat your feet before I get stupid out here." The boys made hurried steps in the other direction, clearly wanting no parts of the young lady holding the big gun.

She moved down Jefferson Avenue taking note of, but not making eye contact with any of the locals. The less they remembered about her, the better. A brown-skinned dread with a heavy accent came at her trying to push up and sell her some weed at the same time. All it took was a look from Frankie and he backed off. Near the end of the block, she found the building she was looking for and ducked inside.

The interior of the building was just as shabby as the exterior. Empty cigarette boxes and cigar fillings littered the floor of the lobby, turning into a damp mess from the snow that had been tracked from the outside. Frankie jogged up the dilapidated stairs, praying they wouldn't collapse under her weight. When she got to the top floor, she knocked on a brown door in a rhythm and waited. There was the sound of bolts being slid free and the door opened. Duce stood there to greet her with open arms.

"Damn, I was beginning to worry about you," he said,

hugging her. "None of these niggaz give you any grief did they?"

"Baby, you know Frankie hold her own," she pulled the Desert Eagle halfway out of her coat pocket so Duce could see the butt.

"Bring your crazy ass in here," he stepped back so she could enter.

Frankie was thoroughly surprised when she stepped into the apartment. The building looked like it would fall over under a strong enough gust of wind, but the apartment itself was plush. The place had soft, lavender carpet stretching from one end to the other and high ceilings. He escorted her into the living room where he had a nice leather sectional and an entertainment system that housed a 42 inch television. Attached to the television were a Play Station 3 and an X-Box 360. *Typical of a dude*, she thought to herself. Duce motioned for her to have a seat and disappeared into the bedroom. He came back out a few seconds later with a blunt between his lips.

Frankie slipped her coat off and took a seat on the sofa. "I see you still love the Mary Jane," she nodded at the blunt.

He lit the blunt and took two deep pulls. "Some things never change," he said, exhaling the smoke. Duce flopped on the sofa next to Frankie and grabbed the remote off the coffee table. He clicked on the CD player and switched the disc to track number two. Lyfe Jennings' *Stick Up Kid* came softly through the speakers.

"That's my shit," Frankie said, humming along with the song.

"You know, I used to lie in my cell and think about you whenever I heard this song," he told her, tipping the ash into the ashtray before handing Frankie the blunt.

"Stop trying to gas me up," she giggled and took a baby pull off the blunt. Frankie immediately started coughing and handed it back to Duce.

"Better be careful with that, this ain't no back yard boogie," he teased her.

"Shut up," she slapped him playfully on the leg, sending a warm sensation through Duce. "The only time you probably thought about me was when you were beating your dick!"

"Nah, I thought about you all the time, even when I was trying so hard not to. Frankie, that shit was killing me knowing that I might never see you again unless it was in a prison visiting room," he saw her face take a saddened look and touched her cheek. "No need to dwell on that anymore though. We're back together and I don't ever plan on leaving you again."

"Don't say it unless you mean it," she warned him.

"Baby, you don't know how much I mean it," Duce kissed her. It was a soft kiss at first, but soon grew more intense. Before either of them knew it, they had spilled onto the floor and were trying to tear each other's clothes off. Frankie and Duce made love on the living room floor, then enjoyed each other on the kitchen counter. When they had finally managed to make it to the bedroom, all they had the strength to do was hold each other

Frankie looked at Duce in the dim light of his bedroom. He was trying to look peaceful but his face held a worried expression. "What're you thinking about?" she asked, moving to lay her head on his chest.

"Give you three guesses," he stroked the back of her head.

"So, you're really going through with it?" she asked, hoping that he might've changed his mind.

"Yeah, after we take off that armored truck, I'm putting Cowboy to bed."

"Duce, you know it's not too late to walk away. I know where Cowboy keeps most of his money stashed and we can rob his ass blind and disappear," she tried to give him an out.

"Oh, I'm gonna take his money. His life is just an added bonus," Duce sat up and moved her so that she was looking up at him. "Frankie, I don't know how comfortable I am with you playing a role in all this. Maybe you could go stay with your brother until it's over with."

She looked at him as if he was crazy. "And risk something happening to you? I don't think so. I'm riding this train to the last stop."

"Your head is *so* fucking hard," he laughed.

"You're one to talk," she shot back playfully. "I guess you gotta do what you gotta do."

"I guess so."

"Duce…"

"Shhh," he placed a finger over her lips. "In a few days all this shit is gonna be over and I'm either gonna be dead, or we're gonna be off somewhere sipping the best of shit and lying in the sun. For now, let's not talk about Cowboy or killing, I just wanna enjoy my time with you."

Frankie nodded and put her head back on his chest. She had so many things running through her mind that she didn't know whether she was coming or going. It was obvious that there was no changing Duce's mind so all she could do was be there for him when the shit hit the fan. Frankie lie there, listening to the sound of Duce's heartbeat until sleep finally took her.

# NINETEEN

**The snow had been falling for three days** straight, and from the looks of things it wouldn't be letting up anytime soon. The ground was covered at least to the ankle with soft frost which was dotted with dirty gray foot prints from all the people milling about downtown Brooklyn. As the saying went, it would be a white Christmas.

Bobby Steward leaned against the side of the armored cube truck, with one hand resting on his sidearm and the other one cupping a Newport in an attempt to keep the falling snow from wetting the cigarette too bad. He tapped his foot impatiently casting an occasional glance at his watch, as if he had somewhere better to be. He had been working for Armored Services for just over two weeks and he was already fucking up. His job had been to stay behind the wheel of the truck while Mike and Aaron gathered the money from inside Macy's, but his yearn for nicotine caused him to disobey the order. He reasoned that no one would be stupid enough to try and take off an armored truck; things like that only happened on television. Besides, if someone did try anything they'd have to deal with Stringer and the double action shotgun that he kept in the back of the truck with him.

His attention was drawn to a statuesque woman making her way to the exit from inside the store to where they were parked. In one hand, she carried at least four shopping bags. A stack of boxes was balanced in the other, obscuring nearly her entire upper body with the exception of her face. She had coffee brown skin and wore her hair in a long black weave that came down her back. Bobby couldn't see her body due to the boxes, but he was able to admire the long legs that stretched down from her short gray skirt. If the rest of her was as built as her legs, there was some lucky stud out there that Bobby wished he could trade places with.

A few paces behind the woman were Mike and Aaron, carrying four heavy bags and laughing about something that Bobby wasn't quite sure of. No doubt they were enjoying the view as they could see the woman's body better than Bobby could. "Lucky bastards," he cursed under his breath.

When the woman reached the double doors, she found that she couldn't pull them open because of all the stuff she was carrying. Never one to miss an opportunity for a free peek, Bobby tossed his cigarette and stepped into the foyer. Smiling like a shyer cat, Bobby opened the doors for her. "Let me get that for you," he said, executing a half bow.

"Aren't you the sweet one," the woman smiled from behind the dark glasses she was wearing. She stepped passed Bobby, giving him a full view of her delicious ass. "Sweetie, I hate to be a bother, but could you get the other doors for me too?" she asked in her most innocent voice.

"But of course," he said, scrambling to pull the last set of doors open for her. He was so caught up in trying to impress the beautiful woman that he didn't even notice when she let the bags drop to the floor and produced a small Uzi.

"You just hold that pose," she hissed, jamming the Uzi into his gut. She made sure to keep her back to the other two Armored Service guards so they wouldn't know what was going on until it was too late. When Bobby tried to make eye contact with his partners, she dug the nose of the gun into his belly with so much force that he gave a small yelp. "If you even think about it, this shit is gonna go from a robbery to a homicide." Though Bobby couldn't see her eyes behind the glasses, something told him that she was serious.

"Now, just keep smiling and back out like you're holding the door for me," she said with ice in her voice. Not wanting to lose his life on Christmas Eve, Bobby did as he was told.

Mike and Aaron's laughter was halted abruptly when they noticed that Bobby wasn't at his post behind the wheel. "What the fuck is this kid doing?" Mike asked Aaron.

"Trying to lose his fucking job," he shifted the bags he was carrying all into one hand so he would be free to draw his weapon if there was trouble. "We're carrying a fucking mint and he's trying to mack, that stupid son of a bitch."

"I'm ratting his ass out when we get back to base," Mike said seriously. As they got closer to Bobby, they noticed that his face was wearing a strange expression. Most 22-year olds would've been smiling from ear to ear in the presence of a stallion like the one he was talking to, but Bobby wasn't. He looked afraid. The two men must've sensed the same thing because they reached for their weapons at the same time. Before either of them could clear their weapons, a voice stopped them.

"Don't be no hero," Cos said, appearing out of thin air. He was wearing a black suit. Like Frankie, glasses covered his angular face, but his hand was jammed under a box used to pack long stemmed roses. "Now, you finish the motion if you want to and we'll see if these are flowers inside this box or iron."

"Why don't you let us help you with those," Duce said, coming from the opposite side. His suit was midnight blue with black pinstripes. At his side, he held a .45. With little to no effort, he took the bags Aaron was carrying while his partner took Mike's. "You boys just keep walking like we ain't even here. And if you think about trying something, we ain't got no problem letting these things go." Cos jiggled the box, "Feel me?" Mike and Aaron nodded dumbly. "Good."

The four men walked through the doors of Macy's like old buddies shopping together. The robbers flanked Mike and Aaron as they stepped through the double doors and onto the snow-covered sidewalk. Both of the guards shot Bobby a murderous look, but no one said anything. If they lived through the robbery they would settle up with him later.

Cos gave Frankie a wink as he passed. She spared a minute to smile at him and when she did Bobby made a move. Out of fear more than bravery, he grabbed Frankie's gun. While he was trying to wrest it from her, the Uzi went off perforating the ground with small holes. One of the bullets bounced off the sidewalk barely missing Duce, but striking Aaron in the leg. Bobby tried to use his weight against Frankie but it backfired when she caught him with a hip toss. The stunned guard hit the snow-packed ground and lied there in a daze.

At the sound of gunfire, Stringer popped the rear doors of the truck with his shotgun at the ready. He moved to train it on the robbers but something crashed into the side of his face. He screamed like a girl as his jaw collapsed like rotten fruit. Through the haze of pain, he could see a hulk of a man in a green suit standing over him holding a very large sledge hammer.

"What're you a fucking idiot?" Thor asked, before he brought the hammer down again. This time the arm closest to the fallen shot gun was crushed by the hammer. "You move again and I'm gonna bust your fucking head open!" He didn't have to worry about that, Stringer was in too much pain to do anything but cry.

"Let's get the fuck outta here!" Cos barked, as he

pushed Mike roughly to the ground. Mike thought about going for his gun, but seeing what happened to his partners he decided it would be smarter just to stay very still.

A brown Plymouth came to a screeching halt beside the armored truck. Cowboy, behind the wheel dressed in a black turtleneck sweater and dark glasses, stuck his head out the window. "I said don't shoot unless you had too. The pigs are gonna be all over this place in a hot minute. Let's move people!" he shouted.

"Hold on, man, we gotta get the money out of the truck," Thor said, reaching for the doors.

"Don't be fucking greedy, Thor. The police are gonna be on our asses any second and I don't look forward to spending my Christmas in the fucking bull pens. Move!" Cowboy ordered.

Thor mumbled something and lumbered to the car with his three accomplices in tow. No sooner than the last of the robbers had climbed into the car several blue and white police cars came racing up the street. Cowboy threw the car into gear and slammed his foot on the gas. Tires squealed showering bystanders with snow before they shot down Livingston Street.

"Didn't I tell you mutha fuckas no gun play?" Cowboy asked, yanking the wheel from left to right to avoid cars and people.

"It was Frankie's fault, she let that nigga get the drop on her," Thor accused, wiping the blood of his hammer with his jacket.

"Fuck you, you fat son of a bitch. You weren't there, so how the fuck would you know what happened?" Frankie asked, pulling off the black wig, exposing her own hair which was braided beneath it

"We can point fingers later, we've got company," Cowboy said, craning his neck to look out the rear window.

Two police cars were hot on their asses and closing the distance at an alarming rate.

"We gotta shake these niggaz," Duce said, clutching his .45 tighter than he needed too. He didn't know if it was the impending assassination of their leader, or the fact of knowing that if they got caught there would be no beating this charge, but he was nervous as hell.

"I got this," Frankie said, taking the shotgun from the rose box and hanging out the rear window. Of everyone in the car, Frankie was the best shot. Her late father was a police officer and had taught her how to shoot a gun at an early age. Bracing the shotgun against her shoulder, she pulled the trigger. The windshield of the first police car shattered causing them to spin out. Another blast shredded their radiator taking them out of the chase, but the second car was still following.

"Come on, boo. They're still on us!" Cowboy said, nearly missing a woman who was crossing the street with her children.

"Hold this mutha fucka steady so I can do my thing," she said, trying to draw a bead on the police car which was swerving in and out of traffic just as expertly as they were. "That nigga is good, but I'm better." Frankie fired off another blast, but this time she wasn't aiming at the police car. The round hit the windshield of a bus that was pulling out in traffic, wounding the driver. The bus swerved and crashed at an awkward angle blocking the entire street. "Told you," she said triumphantly.

Everyone in the car let out a breath of relieve. Duce looked back through the shattered windshield and watched the smoking bus and police lights shrink in the distance. He was glad that they had escaped, but even more so because the police hadn't killed Cowboy before he had gotten a chance to. Cowboy gotten away with money, but Duce would get away with the prize.

# TWENTY

**Cos was up with the chickens that morning,** busting his ass to go meet Cowboy. Their leader had given them all instructions to meet at his place so they could split the take from the Macy's robbery. Because of the brave/stupid security guard, they didn't get what they planned but they'd still snagged $175 grand, giving them $35,000 a piece. He wouldn't be retiring anytime soon, but it was still a respectable haul.

It was already 7:30 a.m. and Thor still hadn't arrived at Cos' place. When his Honda had mysteriously broken down on him the night before, Cos called Thor and asked if he would swing by the crib and snatch him, but as usual Thor was late. "Fucking idiot," Cos mumbled, checking the clip of his .45. He figured he'd give the big man ten more minutes before he jumped in a cab.

Cos settled in his recliner and clicked on his big screen television. It was the latest in Hi-Def technology. Just one more perk to leading a life of crime. The morning news was on and, as usual, it was depressing as hell. After seeing something about a little girl who had been killed by her mother's jealous boyfriend, he shut the television off. It was Christmas morning and he didn't need something like that ruining his mood for the day.

Cos was about to go into the kitchen and grab a cup of

coffee before calling a cab when there was a loud knock at his door. He never had visitors, especially unexpected so he unholstered his gun before creeping to the door. Cos had made it within a few feet of the door when it came crashing in. A swarm of blue uniforms flooded his apartment, shouting and brandishing weapons.

"Drop the gun and eat the fucking floor!" one cop shouted, pointing his gun directly at Cos. The cop's hand shook nervously making Cos wonder if he would shoot him by accident. Knowing when he was facing insurmountable odds, Cos dropped to his knees and raised his hands over his head. The cops wasted no time tackling him roughly to the ground.

"Take it easy, I'm not resisting," Cos said as the cop shoved his knee into his back harder than he needed to.

"The other one isn't here," one of the officers said after a quick examination of the bedroom.

"What the hell is going on here?" Cos asked.

"Costello Brown, we have a warrant for your arrest," the lead officer informed him.

"What the fuck for?"

"For armed robbery and accessory to murder."

Cos' eyes got as wide as saucers as he instinctively calculated the time he'd be facing. He was a notorious thief, so he could understand the robbery, but the murder baffled him. "Hold on, man, you've got the wrong guy!" Cos pleaded.

"Well, we have a witness that says differently," the officer said in a smug tone. The police lifted Cos roughly from the ground and dragged him from his apartment.

Cos' mind raced trying to think of anything that he might have done wrong to have him in such a fucked up predicament but, when you had done as much dirt as he had, there was no way to tell. The only thing he could do is keep his mouth closed and wait to see what happened.

Thor sped through the streets of Harlem cursing himself and the bitch that had made him late on such an important day. He just hoped that Cos wouldn't be too mad at him when he got there. As soon as he bent the corner of Cos' block, his jaw dropped. There were at least five vehicles and fifteen officers milling about in front of his building. He slouched in his seat and coasted by to see what was going on.

In the center of the sea of blue was Cos. His hands were cuffed and there were two cops wearing shit-eating grins escorting him to one of the cruisers. Cos made eye contact with the big man, but didn't stare. Thor knew without having to be told that he needed to reach Cowboy with all possible haste.

"That was some stupid shit, Frankie!" Cowboy yelled, holding his drenched cell phone between his fingers.

"Baby, you don't have to curse at me. It's not like I did it on purpose." She had been in the kitchen doing the dishes and talking to her brother on the phone when she *accidentally* dropped Cowboy's phone in the sink.

"It was still some stupid shit. I don't know why you were on my phone anyway," he placed the cell on the radiator hoping that it would help.

"Because the battery is dead on mine, and your ass is too cheap to get a land line," she shot back.

Cowboy wanted to slap the shit out of her, but a fight with Frankie was the last thing he needed that morning. The last time they had gotten into it, he winded up having to go to the hospital to be treated for the gash on his head she had given him when she hurled a lamp at him.

"Why don't you make yourself useful and go down to the pay phone to call Cos and Thor. They should've been here by now," Cowboy told her.

"Cos called while I was on the phone and said they'd be here in a little while," she lied. The only person she had spoken to other than her brother that morning had been Duce telling her that Cos and Thor would be detained. The night before, he had sabotaged the engine on Cos' Honda. Cos had called Duce and asked him for a ride to the meeting, but he fed him an excuse, leaving only Thor to pick him up. They were going to be quite surprised when the police rushed them on the way out.

"Well, in the meantime, why don't you make a nigga something to eat!" he yelled.

"I got something for you to eat you sneaky piece of shit," Frankie mumbled. Cowboy was about his paper and had plenty of it, which was the main reason she dealt with him, but he had no idea how to treat a lady. She didn't know how she had managed to put up with him for as long as she had, but thanks to Duce, she wouldn't have to do so much longer.

Cos leaned against the wall in the police precinct wearing his best ice grill. There were four other men in the room with him, all holding large index cards with numbers scribbled on them. The police had questioned him for over an hour, but he remained perfectly silent. They were insinuating a million and one things, but the more they spoke the more confident he became that they didn't have anything on him. The thing that he found to be strange was the fact that they kept asking him about Thor. Only Cowboy, Duce and Frankie knew that he was supposed to pick him up that morning, so one of them had to be the leak. No matter whom it was, he was going to make it his business to kill them once he was back on the streets.

The police popped shit and made threats, but none of it moved Cos. He had been in and out of jail far too long to let their empty threats rattle him. He refused to utter anything other than "I want to see my lawyer." Only when his lawyer arrived did he agree to participate in the lineup to prove that they had the wrong man…or so he hoped.

Behind the two-way mirror, the lead detective, who had rushed his house, sat with a young woman. She fidgeted nervously in the hard plastic chair staring at the five men on the other side of the looking glass. She had never seen any of them before, but had been given a description of the man she was to point out during the lineup.

"That's him," she said, pointing at Cos.

"Are you sure?" the lead detective asked.

"Yes."

"This is bullshit," Cos' lawyer threw his hands in the air. "This woman is a prostitute with a rap sheet a mile long. How the hell is she credible?"

"Because she was there," the lead detective told him. "Your boy Brown is a notorious piece of shit and the thing that happened at the Doll House is right up his alley. Now, instead of sitting here slinging insults, I suggest you start trying to convince him to take the deal the DA is sure to offer him for the other four perps."

"This is a miscarriage of justice and I won't stand for it!" the lawyer said animatedly.

"Then sit down," the lead detective said, turning his attention back to the woman. "Now, take a good look honey and there's no need to be scared because he can't see you. Is that the man you saw at the Doll House?"

"Yes, that's him," she said wondering if the detective

was telling the truth about the mirror. "I was tending bar that night and I remember seeing him lurking around the door before the shooting started."

"Okay sweetie, we'll have one of the officers outside take you home. Thank you for your time."

The woman nodded and left the room. What she had told the police was half true. The woman had been the bartender at the Doll House the night Cos and the others had robbed it, but she didn't see his face. Duce had paid her a small ransom to say otherwise. Of course, she would be nowhere to be found when it was time to testify, which would more than likely make Cos a free man, but this was how Duce had planned it. He didn't want his one-time friend gone…just out of the way long enough for him to whack Cowboy.

Cos was less than pleased to find out that he had been fingered as one of the robbers at the Doll House, but he managed to maintain his cool. He needed to keep a clear head in light of the situation. He knew that no one other than the stripper he had tipped had gotten a good look at him, and there was no way his own little cousin would drop a dime on him, leaving only the members of his crew. He and Thor were like brothers so that left Duce, Cowboy and Frankie. Either one or all three of them would pay for turning on Costello Brown.

His lawyer sat waiting for him behind a conference table, while a uniformed officer stood outside the door. As soon as he sat down, the lawyer immediately went into his spiel about how he was going to do everything in his power to free Cos but was waved silent. "Nix the bullshit because I'm not really in the mood to hear it," Cos said, leaning in to whisper. "This is what you're gonna do. Get my cell phone out of my personals as soon as you can. Send big brother a text telling him that there's a weasel in the hen house. He'll know what it means." Without waiting for the lawyer to respond, Cos returned to the conference room door and yelled for the officer to take him back to his cell.

Whoever was behind the set up was sure to have covered their bases so there probably wasn't much he could do other than wait for his arraignment and play it from there. But whoever the traitor was would soon find out that Cos wasn't without his own resources.

# TWENTY-ONE

**"Damn it, Frankie, don't you hear the door?"** Cowboy asked, standing over Frankie who was lounging on the sofa.

"It ain't for me," she said, not bothering to look up from the magazine she was thumbing through.

"I don't know what the fuck has gotten into you lately, woman," he said, heading for the front door.

"Nine and a half inches of paradise," she mumbled.

"What the fuck did you just say?" he stopped short.

"I'm talking about the magazine. I said this bitch gives horrible advice," she lied. "What the hell is your problem this morning?"

"My problem is that I've got almost 200 grand down in the trunk of my car and ain't nobody breaking the door down to try and get their piece. Where the fuck is these niggaz at?"

"Relax, baby, that's probably them at the door now. Their simple minded assess was probably out chasing ass all night."

"I don't give a fuck what they were doing. When I tell niggaz eight o'clock I mean eight o'clock, not a quarter to nine." Cowboy snatched the door open to find only one of his missing soldiers. "At least one of you niggaz has got some sense of time, even if you are half an hour late," he said letting Duce into the apartment.

"Sorry about that, man. I'm just not used to getting up this early no more," Duce gave him a pound and flopped in one of the four folding chairs Cowboy had set up in the living room. Frankie glanced at him, and went back to her magazine. "So, where's everybody else?"

"Damned if I know," Cowboy said, lighting a cigarette. He exhaled a cloud of smoke and began pacing the floor. "Thor, I could understand being a fuck up but it ain't like Cos to be late, especially knowing the kind of paper we got on the ball."

"Maybe they're caught in traffic. The snow had shit moving mad slow," Duce suggested.

"Maybe, but I doubt it. Something doesn't feel right."

"Cowboy, you're going to wear a hole in that carpet. Try to relax," Frankie grabbed his hand to stop him from pacing. Just seeing her touch Cowboy made Duce want to pop the both of them, but he was too close to let his emotions throw it all to shit. He locked his heart in an iron box and focused on the plan.

"I can't relax, baby. I know if I was supposed to get my piece of this big ass haul I'd have been on time. Men like Cos and Thor don't bull shit over bread."

"Cowboy, I'm gonna fix y'all some drinks, maybe that'll calm your nerves," Frankie said, making her way to the mini bar.

"Thanks, baby," he patted her on the ass as she passed. "Duce," he addressed the young man, "there's nothing like having a good woman in your corner. I can always count on Frankie when the chips are down."

Duce gritted his teeth. "I know what you mean. Back before I went to prison, I had a down ass bitch in my corner. She was a straight gangsta," he glanced at the kitchen and then back at Cowboy.

"Yeah, I forgot Cos said you were fresh out of the can, but he never got in to the specifics."

Duce shrugged. "Ain't much to tell. I went down on a bull shit charge that they couldn't make stick."

"So, you were a body catcher, huh?" Cowboy sized him up, wondering if he was bullshitting or not.

"I was one of the best, until a rat set me up." There was now a chill to Duce's voice that made even Frankie nervous.

"Two bodies and you only caught five years? How'd you manage to swing that?" Cowboy asked curiously. Frankie had just returned and set two glasses of Hennessy and Coke on the coffee table. Though Duce was sitting perfectly calm, there was something in his eyes that made Cowboy nervous.

"Wasn't that hard," Duce turned his glass up and downed it. "See, a lot of people owed me favors in the world and I called in every last one. A few well-placed dollars," Duce spread his arms, "and here I am."

"So, you plan on getting back at the cats that tried to shit on you?" Cowboy asked, leaning back on the sofa across from where Duce was sitting.

"Already got the ball rolling," Duce leaned in, staring Cowboy in the eye. "There's just one loose end I gotta tie up to complete the circle." Duce went for his pistol, but before he could draw it, Cowboy had produced a 9mm from beneath the cushion of the couch.

"Try me if you want, but your brains will be out of your head before that gun gets outta your jacket," Cowboy hissed. "You know, you almost got away with it, son. Had you not felt the need to stroll down memory lane I might not have put two and two together until it was too late, D-Murder."

"Bravo, cock sucker," Duce clapped, "but it still doesn't change the fact that you're going to die," he snarled.

"D, you're even stupider than your lame ass brother was. I'm the one holding the pistol, so it looks like you're gonna do the dying," Cowboy gave a throaty laugh, but it was abruptly cut short by the feeling of cold steel against his temple.

"I'll take that, baby," Frankie said, pressing a .38 against Cowboy's temple. He just looked at her in shock as Frankie plucked the gun from his hand.

"You dirty bitch!" Cowboy trembled with rage.

Frankie walked over and sat in Duce's lap with both guns trained on Cowboy. "Not a dirty bitch," she kissed Duce on the lips, but her guns never left Cowboy. "A gangsta bitch. Had I known you were responsible for taking the only thing I've ever loved in this world, I'd have murdered your bitch ass long before today," she kissed Duce on the lips and turned lifeless eyes to Cowboy. "I'm gonna enjoy watching you die, nigga."

No sooner than the words left Frankie's mouth the front door came crashing in. Thor stood in the wreckage of what had been Cowboy's front door with his hammer in one hand and a .40 cal in the other. He had been on his way to Cowboy's when he got the text from Cos' phone. His intentions had been to tie all three of them up and beat a confession out of the traitor, but seeing Frankie sitting on Duce's lap, he had all the proof he needed. Once again a bitch had put a monkey wrench in the works, but he was going to deal with them accordingly.

At the same time Frankie moved to fire at Thor, Duce was trying to get up to draw his own weapon which caused them to collapse back into the chair awkwardly. Thor licked two shots before diving into the kitchen. The first one hit the wall, but the second one nicked Duce's shoulder. Frankie fired at the kitchen with one gun and at Cowboy with the other, but he was able to slip behind the couch.

Duce tossed Frankie to the floor and drew his 9mm, alternating aim between the kitchen entrance and the couch where Cowboy had disappeared. He nodded towards the couch while he moved slowly towards the kitchen. Frankie understood what he meant and began creeping across the living room.

Duce crept along on the balls of his feet moving as silently as he could. He knew Frankie had his back, but couldn't help but to keep looking in the direction where Cowboy had disappeared. It was during one of those nervous glances that Thor popped out of the kitchen. Duce had barely thrown himself to the floor when large chunks of the wall came away in a spray of plaster. Duce fired from a laying position, missing Thor but punching holes in the refrigerator.

Faster than was probably wise, Duce sprang to his feet. The room swam for a minute, but his grip on the gun never wavered. The abrupt fall coupled with the searing gash in his shoulder made his whole arm feel numb. He flexed his fingers around the handle of the gun and began creeping towards the kitchen.

Duce leaned against the outer wall of the kitchen and breathed deeply. He held the gun pointed at the ground in a two-handed grip and pressed his cheek against the wall. By now, someone had surely called the police at the sound of gunfire so he and Thor's game of cat and mouse would have to end sooner than later. Tired of being on the defensive, Duce went on the offensive and stepped into the kitchen.

Sweat from Frankie's palms made the guns feel like

they would slip from her hands with the slightest of movements. She could hear movement in the kitchen but forced herself to focus on her target. Her eyes darted from the spot on the couch that Cowboy had disappeared behind to the end of it. The last thing she needed was for him to go kamikaze and get the drop on her. The sound of gunfire from the kitchen caused Frankie to whirl instinctively, which was a bad move. When she turned back around, Cowboy was popping up from behind the couch, now holding the .357 that she dumbly forgot he kept stashed there.

"You stinking bitch, I'm gonna kill you!" he shouted, firing the cannon.

Frankie hit he floor a split second before the couch exploded in a shower of cotton and springs. "Not in this life time, mutha fucka," she rolled over on her back, firing at Cowboy with the guns. He moved with the speed of a jungle cat, but he wasn't faster than a bullet. He howled in pain as one of the shots tore through his forearm.

"I can't believe you fucking shot me!" he cried from behind the couch. The bullet has passed through, but the arm would be useless.

"Believe it, I told you Frankie Five Fingers don't bluff," she shot back, getting to her knees. She wasn't foolish enough to stand up and make an easier target of herself.

"Frankie baby, it ain't gotta go down like this. We a team, ma. Me and you against the rest of these suckers, right?"

"That me and you shit went out the window when your true colors came out. You should've kept it real with me Cowboy, because then I might've shown mercy, but ain't no sunshine now, baby. This is the final curtain, so get out here and take your bow."

"Oh, it's like that?" Cowboy asked, his voice thick with emotion. "Well fuck you then!" Cowboy started shooting blindly through the couch trying to get at Frankie. She fell on her ass, dropping one of her guns and scuttled backward across the living room. The entertainment system showered her with glass as one of the mad man's bullets struck it. Frankie didn't dare breathe until she had crawled safely behind the wall where Duce had disappeared.

The impact from Thor's hammer sent shockwaves up Duce's wrists. The gun clanged to the ground leaving Duce stunned and unarmed. Instead of shooting him, Thor slammed the handle of his hammer into Duce's jaw. Duce staggered but didn't fall. Thor tried to bring the hammer around for the killing blow, but Duce sidestepped it seconds before it burrowed into the kitchen tiles. In the moment that it took Thor to free the hammer, Duce was on him.

Duce hit Thor with a series of combinations and kicks, but the big man held his feet. He tried to bring his gun arm around, but Duce grabbed it and held on for dear life. Thor tried to swing the hammer, but there wasn't enough room in the kitchen to do so. The big man roared and repeatedly slammed Duce from the oven to the refrigerator but still he held on.

Duce slammed his fist into Thor's jaw as hard as he could, but the big man only got angrier. Dropping the hammer, he grabbed Duce in a bear hug and began to apply pressure. Duce could only yelp because Thor had squeezed too much air out of him for a scream. Seeing the look of pain on Duce's face, the big man applied more pressure, triumphantly laughing at the sounds of Duce's bones cracking.

Duce tried to fight the big man off but he was too strong. Spots suddenly began to flash before his eyes as he felt the first tugs of unconsciousness. If he blacked out in

Thor's grasp, it was over before he got to Cowboy. Something gleaming on the kitchen counter gave Duce hope. He leaned his body as far to the left as he could without helping Thor break his spine and wrapped his hand around the object. With all the strength he had left, he plunged the steak knife into Thor's shoulder.

The sharp pain made the bigger man drop his prey. Duce lay on the ground gasping. He tried to stand, but his legs wouldn't cooperate. Through a haze, he saw the rage in Thor's eyes and knew that it was just about over for him. Thor's huge hands grabbed for the knife protruding from his shoulder blade, but the constant flow of blood made it hard to grab. Eventually getting a grip on it, he yanked the knife free with a roar, sending blood spattering all over the wall. Thor looked at the knife as if it had been an irritating splinter then turned the same glare to Duce.

"I was just gonna shoot you and make it quick, now I'm gonna break as many bones as I can before I finish you off." Thor had taken two steps in Duce's direction when his chest exploded in a spray of blood. He temporarily forgot about Duce and began to grasp at the wound in his chest. He took one more step towards Duce when his head exploded like a rotten melon. The big man's body crashed to the ground rattling the dishes.

Frankie stood in the mouth of the kitchen looking from Duce to Thor. Blood ran from what used to be the man's head onto the kitchen floor and tickled the edges of the carpet. Most women would've probably thrown up at the sight of so much blood and brain matter, but not Frankie. She just stared at the body with her gun still trained on his back.

"You good?" she asked, extending her hand to Duce.

"Yeah, I'll be okay," he allowed her to help him up. "Thank you, baby," he hugged her. Duce inhaled Frankie's scent and let it take him to that special place that only they occupied. He nestled his nose in her hair and for a moment forgot where they were and why they came, until the pain hit. Duce never heard the shot, but he felt it…Lord did he feel it. A white hot fire shot up through his back and spread throughout his limbs. He slumped to his knees leaving a trail of blood on Frankie's chest. Frankie knelt beside Duce, who was breathing heavily.

"Baby, talk to me," she patted his face.

"I knew I should've made you stay home," he tried to tease, but only ended up coughing blood in her face. "My bad," he tried to raise his arm to his mouth to wipe the blood off but couldn't quite manage.

"I'm gonna call an ambulance," Frankie pulled her cell out, but Duce grabbed her by the wrists.

"And tell them what? I got shot trying to kill your boyfriend over a five-year-old murder?"

"What should I do?" she asked frantically.

"Just hold my hand, baby. Sit by me for a minute and let me think about how it used to be."

Frankie looked down at him, dropping tears on his face. She couldn't believe after all this time she was going to lose him again. "Duce…"

"Don't talk baby, just be with me for a minute," he pleaded. Duce's body stiffened as a shock ran through him and then he was still. Frankie placed her ear to his chest but there was only silence.

"Duce, talk to me," she shook him. He opened his mouth to speak, but the only thing that came out was blood. "Don't die on me, baby. Don't you dare leave me again after so long!" Frankie pleaded but, as the light faded in his eyes, she knew it was a wrap. Still clutching her lover in her arms, she turned her murderous glare on Cowboy, who was aiming his smoking pistol at her.

Cowboy recognized the look in her eyes and got a firmer grip on his pistol. "By the time you get the notion to do it, I'll been done rocked your pretty ass to sleep. That was some dirty shit, Frankie," he continued, "and even though you tried to put my lights out over this nigga, the sucker in me wants to forgive you. The things I've done and will do in life are fucked up, but that's the G-code, ma. Kill or be killed, you know how it is."

"I hate you, Cowboy. You're a fucking monster," Frankie sobbed.

"You don't mean that," he said emotionally. "I put you in pocket…gave you a purpose, and this is how you carry it?" he couldn't hide the hurt in his voice. "Why Frankie, why do this to the man who you're supposed to love?"

Frankie looked from Duce to Cowboy with tear-filled eyes. "As I sit here watching my heart bleed out on to your kitchen floor, I'm asking myself the same question," Frankie stroked Duce's bloody face.

"Come with me, Frankie," Cowboy extended his hand. "We can work this shit out, ma."

For the first time, Frankie looked directly at Cowboy and he could see the pure hatred in her eyes when she spoke. "Cowboy, if you're gonna kill me, you better get on with it, because as God as my witness as soon as I can get the strength in these limbs, I'm gonna snatch that piece up and kill you," she nodded at her abandoned gun, laying on the floor less than three feet away.

Cowboy looked from the body of his dead enemy to the woman he'd been sharing his bed with all this time. A part of him hoped that he would see those loving and obedient eyes staring back at him, but there was only hate. "Even in death, this faggot still got your heart? So be it, Frankie Five

Fingers." Cowboy's finger touched the trigger, but several red dots appearing on his chest gave him pause. He looked up and when his brain registered what was going on, all the blood rushed to his face.

"You were a fool to steal from me, bandito," El Pogo said from the doorway. Several hard-faced and armed men trained their weapons on Cowboy. "Adios," El saluted him.

"No, no, no!" Cowboy raised his hands, having them blown off in chunks. The first wave of bullets knocked him into the far wall, and the second wave pinned him there. When they finally stopped firing, Cowboy was a little more than a pile of flesh and some clothing. One by one, the men stepped out of the apartment, leaving El Pogo. Without even turning around, Frankie could feel his eyes on her.

"What did you see?" he asked.

"Not a mutha fucking thing," Frankie said, never taking her eyes off Duce. "As a matter of fact, I wasn't even here."

El Pogo nodded. "Let's hope you stick to that, so my people don't have to come looking for you too, Frankie Five Fingers," he said slyly. She didn't miss the threat beneath his words.

Frankie knelt there for a while longer before the reality of her situation set in. She got to her feet and rushed to the closet where she drug out Cowboy's roll-on suitcase. She took the money from the safe, the freezer and several other stash spots Cowboy had in the apartment. Trying to keep her cool, she wheeled it all outside and put it with the money in the trunk of Cowboy's ride. She knew he had several other safe houses where he kept money and jewels, but she would leave that for the scavengers. One thing Frankie always knew was how to cut her losses, Duce had taught her that. Frankie wasn't sure where she would go or what she would do with her new life, but whichever way the wind blew her, she'd do it by herself. Frankie had been blessed and cursed twice in a lifetime, but this time Duce left her with a priceless jewel. A cold heart wasn't hard to mend, it was impossible.


**THE END**

# AN EXCERPT FROM

# *NEXT DOOR NYMPHO* BY CJ HUDSON

# PROLOGUE

POW! Diamond's back slammed against the wall. The impact of her vertebrae crashing into the drywall caused her framed, autographed pictures of basketball player, Darius Jones to shatter onto the hardwood floor. Diamond's life flashed before her eyes as she thought back to all the lives she had ruined; all the marriages she had wrecked in her short time on earth; twenty-five years to be exact. The loud thunder clapping through the skies drowned out her agonizing screams.

Her deadly moment had come. The red hot slug from the .357 Magnum ripped through her right shoulder blade, shredding tissue and bone along the way. The crumbling drywall was no match for the angry bullet as it tore through speedily. It destroyed everything in its path, and caused Diamond to fear for her life. Her heart pounded as she tried desperately to reach the .25 automatic tucked down in her purse. To her surprise, it wasn't there. Suddenly, she looked up through tear soaked eyes and saw her assailant holding the missing pistol.

"Looking for this?"

The shooter's haunting laugh sent chills up and down Diamond's spine. Bleeding profusely, she struggled to stand up.

"Who the fuck is you? What the fuck is this shit all about?" Diamond asked hysterically.

"You've stolen something from me that I can't get back, and now its time to pay the piper," a cold voice whispered.

Diamond was sure that she'd heard the voice before but couldn't quite place it. The shooter was dressed in black jeans, a black pullover hoodie, and black boots with a black fedora hat pulled down over one eye. Diamond looked at the floor in amazement as the .25 automatic slid across the floor to her.

"Go ahead, bitch. Pick it up."

Foolishly, Diamond snatched the gun up, pointed it, and pulled the trigger. The hooded gunman's sinister laugh resonated throughout the room.

"And all this time I thought you were smart. But you're obviously a dumb bitch. You really think I would give your ass a loaded gun? All that cum you've been swallowing has made your ass semi-retarded."

Diamond threw the gun down in disgust.

"Fuck!" she shouted.

"Yep, bitch! That's exactly what you are! Fucked!"

As hard as she tried, Diamond just couldn't get a clear read on the voice that was coming at her. Whoever it was sounded very well educated. There was no slurred speech or slang to connect them with the hood.

"What the fuck is that 'spose ta mean?" Diamond asked.

"It means, it's payback time and there's nothing you can do to stop what's about to happen to you."

Diamond's eyes bulged.

"You've allowed your over-active vagina to ruin your life. You fucked the wrong guy, baby. You took away my life and now I'm gonna return the favor."

Diamond tried to think back, but she'd fucked so many men that she couldn't be sure who the shooter was talking about. Diamond flinched when her assailant pulled something from her back pocket. With a flick of the wrist, a picture sailed across the floor toward her feet. Reaching down with her good arm, she picked it up and stared at it.

"I don't even know this fuckin' kid!" she wailed.

"Well, maybe you should meet him then. The assassin walked stealthily toward Diamond with the barrel pointed at her head. When the hat and glasses were removed, a look of confusion spread across Diamond's face. Then it hit her.

"Wait a fuckin' minute! It's you! But why? You…"

"Your worse fuckin' nightmare, bitch! I would tell you to say hello to him, but he's in heaven. And you're on your way to hell."

Light flashed in Diamond's face as several hollow point bullets were fired. For the first time in her life, Diamond began to pray, and hoped like hell she would survive.

# Chapter One

## *Diamond*

### How it all Began

"Where the fuck these bitches at?" I yelled to no one in particular.

They always crampin' my style with this bein' late bull-shit. Most bitches like to be fashionably late so they can make an entrance, but not me. I like to get there and scope out the product. That way, if I'm not feelin' the spot, or the men then I got time to go somewhere else, and it won't interfere with my dick searchin' time. I thought about drivin' myself and just tellin' Essence and Angie that I would meet them at the club, but then I came to my senses. Gas in Cleveland had soared to damn near four dollars a gallon. *Why the fuck should I drive and use my gas? Fuck that. Let them hoes drive their own shit, I told myself with a smirk.*

I stopped to laugh while checkin' myself in the mirror for the fifth time in the last twenty minutes. No doubt, I was a sexy bitch. I slid my hand across my short, pixie cut, hair style wondering why people couldn't see a touch of Halle Berry in me. Besides our similar hairstyles, we were both curvaceous, same height, same complexion, just different sized wallets. The only other difference was the fact that Halle once had a sex fanatic on her hands, and I in turn craved sex daily.

It was never hard to get my daily dosage 'cause niggas go crazy over Dream, the nickname I'd given my pussy. Like this one nigga I use to fuck around with. I can't even remember his name… but this nigga was actin' like he ain't ever seen pretty, succulent pussy before. Talk about clingy; I couldn't take a shit without him wanting to wipe my ass. The only way I could get rid of the magnet muthafucka was to have Essence and Angie bring him by the house and act as if I had a surprise for him. I had one for his ass alright. As soon as he walked through the door, he was treated with the surprise of seeing my lips wrapped around another nigga's dick. The look on his face was priceless. Essence and Angie laughed for almost an hour behind that shit.

The worst part by far though was that the lame ass nigga didn't even have the self-respect to get mad. He just stood there cryin' like a bitch, askin' how could I do that to him. Now I know that I'm a bad bitch but damn, show some fuckin' dignity. If that situation taught me anything, it taught me that just because a nigga has a big dick doesn't mean that he can fuck.

Suddenly, I stopped thinkin' and rushed over to the window to look out into the darkness. I got annoyed because I still didn't see my girls, or any headlights comin' down the street. Not content with the view, I opened the door, walked on the porch and looked up and down the street. Still, nothing. Starting to get pissed, I flipped open my cell phone to call Angie.

"Yo', where the fuck y'all at, chick?"

"Keep yo' bra on hoe, we coming." Before I could spit out a comeback, Angie hung up on me.

"Bitch!" I shouted. I'ma get the last muthafuckin' laugh on her ass. That chick owes me ten dollars and as soon as she turns her head tonight, I'ma go through her purse and clip her trick ass. That was a promise. Friend or no friend, I never played when it came to money. I didn't have much, so what I had, I needed..

Knowin' that there was nothing else that I could do besides wait, I went into the kitchen and grabbed a bottle of Mango Alizè that I had chillin' in the fridge. After gulpin' down a few swallows, I decided to call Angie's ass back and cuss her out for hangin' up on me. Just as I started to dial, the phone vibrated in my hand. After checkin' the screen and seeing that it was my boss, Jason Sims, I let it go to voice mail.

As much as I loved havin' his white, eleven inch dick blowing my back out, tonight was girl's night out. Plus, I was sure to get a chance to test drive some fresh dick at the club. Dream needed variety. *Maybe I can catch him at work so we can sneak off somewhere. I really wanna suck him off*, I thought with a devious smirk.

I remembered the last time his pale-lookin' ass came over. Me and my girls were just chillin' out, smokin' a fat ass blunt and watchin' Martin re-runs. But as soon as he walked in with a duffle bag slung over his shoulder, I knew what time it was. Fifteen minutes later my girls were out the door and I was gettin' my ass waxed. Damn, just thinkin' about that night got me hot as fuck. As if it had a mind of its own, my right hand found its way to the top of my off the shoulder, metallic looking dress and dove inside. Ever so slowly, my hand slid over my left breast and caressed my size 34 Double D's.

"Oh shit," I inadvertently moaned as I pinched my now swollen nipple.

After bringin' my left hand up to squeeze my right nipple, I let my right hand drop toward the bottom of my dress. Before I knew it, my finger was attacking my clit. Soon after, two fingers found their way inside my wet love hole. I finger fucked myself until both of my fingers were dripping with pre-cum. Wantin' to bust a nut in the worst way, I slid my fingers out of my pussy and guided them back up to my clit. I pinched, messaged, teased, and flicked my little man in the boat until I exploded.

"Oooo, shit that felt good," I moaned to myself as hot cum ran down my honey colored legs, slightly burning my inner thigh.

A voice sounded.

"Bitch, what the fuck you doing?"

Startled, I opened my eyes to see Essence and Angie standing in front of me with smirks on their faces. As usual, Angie's face was perfectly painted with tons of make-up; different color eye shadows, foundation, blush, and mascara that looked as if it would never come off. Her micro braids were pulled up into a tight ponytail.

"The fuck it look like I'm doin', Angie," I shot back, showin' them that I wasn't embarrassed in the least. "You hoes took so long; so I figured I'd get a nut off while I was waitin'."

"Damn, slut. Yo' nympho ass couldn't wait 'til you got back home?" Angie asked with her nose turned up.

"Nympho? Chick, you got a lotta nerve."

"Look, you two can argue in the car," Essence said in her overly proper voice. "Let's roll."

Essence led the way as me and Angie eye-balled each other, headed out the door in search of some hot action.

"And how come yo' ass don't never drive?" Angie had the nerve to ask me.

"Yes, how come you don't ever drive," Essence cosigned.

*Jealous-ass hoes*, I thought. Just as I was about to make up an excuse, I heard a deep, raspy voice call my name.

"Yo' Diamond, can I holla at chu fo' a minute?"

I turned my head to the right to see my neighbor, Paul, starin' at me with puppy dog eyes. Although this muthafucka was really starting to get on my fuckin' nerves, I smiled to myself at the thought of my pussy being so good that it kept on breakin' these weak-ass men down.

"Damn, girl, that nigga still sweating the fuck outta you?" whispered Angie.

Nodding my head and rollin' my eyes, I asked my friends to wait in Essence's whip. Like I knew those nosey bitches would, they let the windows down so they could eavesdrop. "Damn, you hoes nosey," I said, poppin' my lips. They gave me the finger as I turned around and walked toward Paul.

"What, nigga? Don't you see I'm 'bout to kick it with my girls?"

"Yeah...I mean...I just wanna holla at chu fo a second."

"What you want Paul?" I asked, rubbin' my temples like I was gettin' a headache.

"I'm jus' sayin' Diamond...I mean damn, what the fuck I do? I thought we had a good thing going and you just dropped a muthafucka!"

After lookin' at his screwed up face, I broke out into laughter. I know this sucka for love ass nigga don't call his self gettin' mad. Not when after I cut his ass off from the punanny, he cried like a bitch. After I finally stopped laughin', I put my hands on my shapely hips and went into check-a-nigga mode.

"First of all Paul, I told yo ass from the gate, I wasn't lookin' for no serious type shit. I ain't tryin' to be wifey to no muthafucka."

"I'm just sayin', Diamond, I ain't tryin' ta make you wifey, I just wanna keep havin' a good time wit chu."

I can't lie. I thought about goin' one more round in the sack with Paul, my El DeBarge look-alike. The nigga couldn't fuck worth shit, but his tongue game was on point like a mutha-fucka. I quickly dismissed that thought, knowin' that this nigga would get even more sprung if I gave him any more of my killer pussy. Dream was a beast.

"Look, Paul," I said preparin' him for the lie I was about to spit out. "I didn't wanna tell you this but apparently yo ass need to hear it. The reason I stopped fuckin' you is because me and my ex are gettin' back together. I didn't tell you at first be-cause I didn't wanna hurt your feelings, but you keep pressin' me about the shit." I paused to lick my thick lips 'cause I knew that shit turned him on. "Look, I gotta go. My girls gettin' impa-tient. Plus, I don't want my dude to do a ride by and catch me talkin' to you."

Without saying another word, I turned on my heels and headed for Essence's 2009 Nissan Pathfinder. By the time I

jumped in and closed the door, my girls were already crackin'
the fuck up.

"Damn, bitch. You got that fool's nose open wider than
Essence's legs," cracked Angie.

As usual, Essence didn't get bent out of shape. She just
frowned and gave Angie the finger. Her behavior seemed a lil'
weird but I didn't say shit. That was her problem. I had my own
issues to worry about.

"I keep tellin' you bitches that my pussy is the best thing
since hair weave," I said, braggin' on my sweet sex. I took one
last look at Paul's sad ass face as Essence pulled off.

*Umph...pathetic ass nigga.*

Order your copy of Next Door Nympho today!!

# HERE'S MORE EXCERPTS FROM
## *LIFE CHANGING BOOKS...*

# MONEY MAKER
# BY: TONYA RIDLEY

## Chapter One

CLICK.

The cocking sound of Trick's Smith and Wesson shocked everyone around, but especially a frightened Dajon. His face tightened even more as Trick pressed the tip of the gun forcefully into his temple. Dajon laid frozen beneath his sheets panting like an old, overweight dog, breathing loudly through his nose. He had no idea how the trio had crept into his home unseen and unheard in the wee hours of the morning. But he knew the end result. Trick's reputation was known throughout the Philly area, so a save wasn't likely. He watched as Trick gave instructions to his workers who stood guard on both sides of the room, while Trick sat on the edge of the bed close to Dajon's shivering body.

"You want me to bust 'em?" Felony asked in his raspy voice.

Trick nodded slowly as he gazed into Dajon's chubby face. He nodded his head up and down as the street lights shone into the dark bedroom giving Trick a chance to see every fearful expression on Dajon's face. Although the New York Yankees fitted hat hid Trick's scowl, it was clear that his eyes remained focused on Dajon for nearly twenty seconds while his boy's Felony and Polo stared at him in disbelief.

"Yo, like dis taking too long, dawg. Let's go," Polo uttered.

"I got this," Trick countered.

Trick was always difficult to figure out. To most, his calm demeanor was a sign of weakness, but to those who knew him, understood that he was in his most ruthless state when in deep thought... always trying to figure out the best way to take an enemy out. Dajon knew Trick well enough since he'd fronted him drugs on a regular basis. He just didn't know him as well as Felony and Polo did. Suddenly, Dajon's thoughts were cut short. The moment that Trick leaned over, moving closer to Dajon's face, he quickly shut his eyes tightly. Fat boy knew it was over and sadly, there was no escape.

"You see where stealin' gets you?" Trick taunted, pressing the gun even more forcefully into his temple.

Sweat poured from Dajon's face as he pleaded, "C'mon man! I told you what happened...!"

"You must notta heard what happens to niggas who fuck with me, yamean?" Trick said.

"C'mon, man!" Dajon begged even more.

Before he could get another word out of his mouth, Trick withdrew the gun from his head, hitting Dajon across the face with the butt of the gun. Instantly, blood trickled from his face and his eyes ballooned in fear.

"I swear on my daughter, man! Don't do this. Don't do this, man," Dajon ended as tears streamed down the side of his cheek.

"Bitch-ass nigga," Trick sniped.

"Fuck dat shit!" Felony shouted, as he paced back and forth on the right side of the bed. He moved closer to Trick with vengeance in his eyes. "Trick, you know dis nigga lying. Lemme bust'em?" he asked again, only this time he'd removed the .357 that had been stuffed down his loose fitting pants.

Both he and Polo had gotten antsy since they'd been in Dajon's house for more than ten minutes. The plan had called for a quick in and out, leaving Dajon dead. Trick had known for weeks that Dajon's fabricated story about how he'd gotten robbed while in possession of 70,000 dollars worth of Trick's product was all a lie. He'd given him the chance to confess, even offering Dajon a re-payment plan, yet nothing worked. Dajon kept sending messages that Trick should just take it as a loss because there was nothing he could do to get the money back.

Trick finally spoke after minutes of silence. "So Dajon, you know a nigga from the East side name Dre?" He pressed the gun into Dajon's temple once again.

A lump formed in Dajon's throat.

"Ahhhhhhh."

"Huh nigga, you know who I'm talkin' about, right?" Trick jolted the gun a bit. "I got me a sexy lil biddy on the east side so I gotta few friends, yamean?"

"Yeah…I know what you mean, Trick. But c'mon man, put the gun down!" Dajon cried out, while remaining stiffly in place.

"Nah, nigga. You sold my shit to that nigga, thinkin' I wouldn't find out. I know everythin' that goes on in my town," he said with discontent, then grit his teeth. "I own this town. Yamean?" he asked with even more anger in his voice.

Of course, Dajon never said a word. He simply cried like a bitch. Yet none of it phased Trick. He was used to punks and wanna-be hustlers. He'd seen it all his life. In an instant, Trick transformed into what Felony had been waiting for. He rose from the bed like he was being attacked.

Boom!

Trick never even flinched as the gun exploded. But even Felony cringed at the sight of Dajon's blood that covered the crisp white sheets. The sound from the gun left all three men with ringing ears, which of course made Trick realize they had less than a minute to make it to the back of the house where the getaway truck was waiting. Trick had been killing for years so not only was he skilled at murder, but at getting away with it too. It was what he did best. Murder was the name of the game. His whole life consisted of getting money and slaying anybody who got in his way.

Within minutes, Trick had switched into high gear. His jewels glistened in the darkness as he jetted down the stairs, taking two at the time, then out the back door, following on the heels of Felony. He moved swiftly knowing that someone had probably heard the shots. Trick, Polo, and Felony ran like their lives depended on it, rushing toward Trick's 2010 off white Cadillac Escalade. Within minutes, Polo had hopped in the driver's seat, started the ignition, and sped through the alley way, hopping onto Gratz Street. Trick sighed a deep sound of relief as he laid back in his butter soft leather seats, knowing he'd just gotten away with another murder.

Although his bald head was covered in sweat, he was pleased with how things had gone. He knew that with Polo driving he could rest his eyes for a moment while sitting in his second best treasure. The Escalade with deep black tinted windows was every man's dream. It was fully equipped with everything from 12-inch plasma screen TV's, custom black floor mats and a Bose' system which Polo had now pushed to the limit. Plies song, *Wasted* blasted from the speakers as they sped down Broad street.

Although the music pumped, Trick thought deeply about his life. As strange as it sounded, he was tired of the ups and downs of the cocaine game. And definitely tired of the hatin' niggas in the biz. Everybody he'd ever met was cut throat with the exception of Polo and Felony. It was time for a drastic change, he thought to himself. He'd committed to throwing in the towel and sticking to his new money making business…one that would set him straight for a lifetime. Little did Felony know, but Trick was about to separate himself from any dealings with drugs after their last deal they were headed to make.

"Man, like what time we gotta meet up with Ce-lo?" Trick asked Felony.

"9 a.m." Felony laughed.

"Fuck. That's five hours from now." Trick tugged on his long, full beard showing that he'd already gotten restless. "A nigga need some sleep."

"Dat's your boy. The only nigga in town who gotta get up at da crack of dawn to get served."

"Like that nigga better be glad his money right," Trick announced. "Yo, stop me by that 24 hour spot….Ahhh what's that jawn called?" Trick snapped his fingers as Felony made a sharp turn, causing him to hold on to the handle above him. "Richies, that's the name of it. Get me one of them egg sandwiches before we go cook up." He closed his eyes. "And good lookin' out back there."

"Always," both men said in unison.

"Now hurry Felony, a nigga hungry," Trick said slouching down in the seat.

"Gotcha dawg."

For several minutes Polo and Felony laughed and talked shit to one another until Trick's cell phone rang. He opened his eyes knowing what was next. The caller ID read trouble. It was Mena, Trick's money hungry girlfriend.

"Talk to me."

"Im'a talk to you alright. Fuck you, Trick! It's five o'clock in the morning and you still not home! Where the fuck you at?" Mena shouted through the phone.

"Takin' care of business. You know what that means, right?" He smirked. "You wanna spend big money every day…well somebody gotta make it, so chill your foul mouth ass out." He paused and put more bass in his voice. "Aye Mena, I told you about disrespectin' me."

"Fuck you, Trick! I bet if I change the locks on your ass, you'll come home at a decent hour."

"Mena, I got shit to do. And besides, It's not like I'm out with some biddy. So I'll see you about ten. And remember, that's my jawn, bitch. You just on a guest pass."

"Ten? Mufucka, you crazy? She screamed like the devil had possessed her spirit. "See if I'm here when you get here, nigga? That staying out all night shit is a no-no for me."

Trick held his breath and gritted his teeth as he often did when his blood boiled. Mena had a unique way of getting deep under his skin. Even though they'd been together for five months, he wasn't crazy in love. He had other women that he preferred to play house with, and Mena knew it. Trick just wasn't the settling down type…just really wanted his dick sucked the moment he opened his eyes every morning. Although Mena's head game and pussy was on point, she was even better for his newly discovered hustle that had been growing more and more by the weeks.

"Mena, if you stop askin' me for new purses, clothes, and jewelry every day, maybe I could come home more often. Man, bye!" Trick spat.

"Trick, Trick, Trick," Mena called out, still holding the phone, but got no answer.

Just as the call ended, Felony startled everyone in the truck. "Oh shit!" he blurted out glaring at the rear view mirror.

By the time Trick turned to look behind, he could hear the sirens sounding from the rear. The blue and red flashing lights sent him into a fast frozen state. In an instant his heart rate sped, wondering what his next move would be.

# Chapter Two

Five hours had passed and Trick felt like he had conquered the world. He and Felony had been in a fake high-speed car chase, cooked three keys, made the drop to his early morning sale, and now had two large bags of money. It killed him that Ce-lo was his only connection who always wanted to meet early in the morning. Most times, he didn't care. But considering he hadn't gotten any sleep all night this was beyond his limits. He'd killed a man, cooked cocaine like a top chef and was now on his way home to Mena's loud mouth.

After almost falling asleep behind the wheel a few times, Trick finally pulled up in front of his 4,800 square foot home in Gladwyne several minutes later. All he could think about as he turned off the truck's engine was his plush king sized bed that he couldn't wait to dive into. No matter how long he'd been into the fast money drug game, he could never get used to the grueling hours the job required. However, after walking up the driveway his entire demeanor changed as he stopped to gaze at his new prized possession. Gently rubbing his hand across the snow white Bentley Continental GT, he quickly realized that if it wasn't for the work he put in, the new $187,000 dollar car would still be on the showroom floor. He was especially proud of the custom red and black seats and chrome Dub 22 inch rims. As

Trick thought about how his new beauty could go from 0-60 miles per hour in 3.7 seconds, the front door to his house flew open. He didn't even have to look up. He knew exactly who it was.

"I can't believe this! Do you know what time it is?" Mena yelled as she stormed outside barefoot in an oversized RIP Michael Jackson t-shirt.

"Yo, I ain't in the mood for this shit, Mena. Take yo ass back in the house."

"I don't give a damn what you're in the mood for, Trick. It's almost ten o'clock in the morning and you're just getting home!"

Trick looked on as one of his white neighbors pulled out of his garage. He waited for the nosey grey haired attorney to drive off before he gave Mena the look of death. "Mena, you better get the fuck outta my face, yamean? Like don't be tryna cause no fuckin' scene in front of my crib. That's all I need is for one of these white mufuckas to call the cops."

"If you stop coming home at disrespectful hours I wouldn't have to act like this." When Trick bent down to wipe a small speck of dirt off the driver's side door, Mena placed her hands on her curvaceous hips and gave him a stern look. "All you care about is this fucking car. Why do you even want me around if you don't give a shit about me?"

Instead of caving into Mena's latest nagging fest, Trick decided to ignore her. Thinking the silent treatment would work, he turned around and made his way into the house. Not one for giving up, Mena followed him like a trained puppy into their two story family room, never missing a beat.

"So, are you gonna tell me why the fuck I'm even here if you don't care about me?" she continued. "I'm so tired of this!"

"Leave then," Trick replied in a nonchalant tone.

Mena's eyes bulged. "Excuse me?"

"You heard me…leave then. All you do is fuckin' nag me, Mena. After all the shit I been through over the last twelve hours, a nigga don't wanna have to come home to this."

Mena finally calmed down. "I'm sorry. I just…"

"You just what? You just run your fuckin' mouth too much. You have no idea the shit I go through when I'm out in these streets, yamean? Me and my niggas were out there tryna outrun some fuckin' cops who weren't even chasin' us and shit. Then I gotta come home to your ass tryna blast me outside in front of the whole neighborhood. Fuck that. It's plenty of other bitches willin' to take your place, so if you wanna leave…bounce."

Even though Trick talked a good game, he really didn't want Mena to leave. She was street smart and good for the business. Plus, she knew too much about his operation. Fighting with Mena every night over stupid shit was starting to take it's toll on him. Trick sat down in his favorite spot on the couch, which had a slight dent from his massive size. At 6'3, two hundred and eighty three pounds, and a tatted up frame, he constantly reminded everyone of the rapper, Rick Ross.

"You know…I shoulda left you a long time ago when you did that bullshit." Mena's entire mood changed. With water welled up in her eyes, she spoke from the heart, "I mean…anybody else with some sense would've left you Trick! But I stayed! In spite of it all!"

"C'mon Mena, don't go there with that shit again. Yamean? Like, we'll neva agree on how it all went down."

Mena went off! "We, my ass! You did it Trick, and you know it. You fucking did it!" she repeated between sobs. "And I'll never forgive you. She paced the floor and let the tears flow. "I got all this shit bottled up inside me still trying to keep this secret from everyone else. And I'm sick of people asking me about it. I'm tired of lying, Trick!"

"I really don't give a fuck what people think, yamean? Like, let's tell the whole story and let your family decide what really happened that night."

"Fuck you, Trick!" Mena shouted to the top of her lungs.

"Let's do it, bitch! Keep talkin' shit."

For some reason when Trick talked to Mena that way it

turned her on. She was definitely attracted to men who took control, and dismissed anyone who appeared to be weak. Quickly switching up from bitch mode, Mena walked over to Trick and sat down on his lap. Even though she was still emotional about all that had been said, Mena managed to push all those feelings aside for the moment. She dried her tears with the back of her hand, and let a slight smile slip from her moist lips. In reality, no matter how mad she was at him she couldn't leave…not yet anyway.

Moving in directly on *his spot*, Mena circled his diamond encrusted ear with her tongue. She knew the minute he realized she didn't have any panties on, her recent actions would soon be forgiven.

"I'm sorry, baby," she whispered in a seductive tone. "You know everytime I think about that horrible night, I get crazy."

"Yeah. I'm tryna understand you. You just need time to heal, I guess."

It wasn't long before Trick's tense body began to relax. No matter how mad he was, he could never deny her sex. If it wasn't for her Beyonce like hips, C-cup breasts, small waist and bomb-ass dick sucking techniques, she would've been gone a long time ago.

"Like you gotta stop that naggin' shit for real."

Mena nodded her head then kissed Trick's full lips. "I know."

Trick pulled his trademark black t-shirt off, then rubbed his hand through Mena's wavy twenty-two inch weave. Instantly, Mena attacked his chest with her hands. He was far from being chiseled, but it always made him feel sexy when she outlined his battle tattoos with her finger. Reaching for his pants, Mena started rubbing on his dick, which started to rise at the thought of her next move. Trick craved her deep throat action, and compared to any other broad she was second to none.

"Oh, so you're not mad at me anymore?" Mena asked with a slight smile.

Before he could respond, she quickly got on her knees, unzipped his Blac Label jeans then pulled out Trick's growing dick. It wasn't long before she began to suck it like it was her favorite lollipop. Trick's eyes rolled to the back of his head while Mena did her best impersonation of Superhead. Once his dick reached it's full erection, Mena stopped.

"Stand up," she ordered.

Happy to oblige, Trick stood to his feet and watched as Mena attempted to grab his wide ass with both of her hands so that he could fuck her face and show off her deep throat skills. Mena's gag-reflexes were sick, which allowed her to take in all ten inches with no problem. Feeling like he was about to bust, Trick backed up before pulling Mena to her feet. With his size, man handling her 5'8 frame was easy.

"Assume the fuckin' position," he said, stroking his dick.

Knowing exactly what that meant, Mena walked over to the dining room table, lifted up her t-shirt then spread her legs for easy access. Doggy style was both of their favorite positions, especially Mena who loved being able to feel every inch of Trick's meat going deep inside her. Not to mention, he was able to reach her spot much easier.

"Yes, baby fuck this pussy," Mena moaned as Trick began to stroke her with a steady rhythm. "Oh, Daddy, I love this dick."

With his ego being stroked, Trick began to dive even deeper into her walls. He really wanted to punish her for all the stress she'd been putting him through lately. However, the harder he pumped, the more he saw her ass bounce up and down, which made him even hornier. Nobody's ass could clap the way Mena's did.

"Oh, shit I'm about to cum," Trick squirmed.

Never missing a chance herself to put it down, Mena hopped up and turned around so she could lick and suck up all her man's juices. Unleashing all of his frustration and energy, Trick blasted every drop that his cannon could produce into Mena's throat. The feeling was unexplainable as she used her jaws to try and pull out even more.

    *Damn…it's too bad this bitch is always stressing me. She really would be a good broad to keep around,* Trick thought right before he made his way to the bedroom and passed out.

## Money Maker…In Stores Now

# WEALTHY & WICKED
# BY: CHRIS RENEE

## Prologue

My eyes opened wide to the sight of the white ceiling. The bright lights caused a temporary fog as I tried to shake away the numbing pain that exploded in my brain.

"Well, it looks like my patient is awake," the voice said from the other side of the room. I tried to turn my head towards it but I had no strength left in my body.

"What do you mean patient? Where am I?" I couldn't remember much of anything before this moment. I tried my hardest to figure out how she had gotten me in this position.

"You're my patient. And in very good hands." She walked towards me with a long needle in her hand and a sinister smile on her face. I panicked!

"I swear, if you don't let me up from here."

"If I don't let you up, then what?"

"Then, I'll…"

"You won't be doing a damn thing, sweetie. I'm running this show." She laughed at my futile attempt to untie myself.

"This shit isn't funny." I continued to tug at the burlap ropes that had my arms confined to the bottom of the heating pipes.

"This isn't supposed to be funny. Well, maybe it is for me, but I'm sure you won't find any humor in this at all."

"Why arc you doing this?"

"Because bitches like you deserve to lose every now and then. Now, open those legs up wide so I can take what belongs to me."

My heart rate accelerated as the liquid in the needle shot through my arm. I wanted to fight but whatever she pumped my veins with had rendered me paralyzed. "Please, stop! I don't have anything of yours. I swear it's not what you think. Please, just let me explain." Tears flew from the corners of my eyes as she continued to laugh at me. I had to admit, I had done some pretty foul things in my life but I couldn't think of any that would make someone want to do me in like this.

"I'm over wanting to hear an explanation from you. At the end of the day, you did what you did and now you must pay." Her voice took on a stern mother's tone.

"Don't do this, please. I'm begging you! I'll do whatever you want, just let me go." My pleas fell on deaf ears as she started to hum a nursery song. One I'd never heard…it seemed more sadistic than anything.

"For reasons unknown to me, you keep landing on top," she spat. "So, it's only natural that I take matters into my own hands," she whispered in my ear as I began to lose consciousness. "That's right, Tracey, take a deep breath. You never deserved to carry this precious gift, not someone as trifling as you."

Quickly, she started the tedious process of taking what she thought should've been hers in the first place. All I could do was cry and hope like hell that someone would save me. As the cramps rapidly shot through my stomach, I realized that she had come to take my baby.

Pick up your copy today

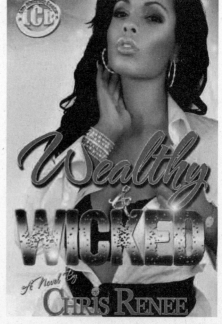

Pick up your copy today

Wealthy & Wicked

A Novel By Chris Renee

A NOVEL BY BEST SELLING AUTHOR
**J. TREMBLE**

*Bedroom*
**GANGSTA**

Seven, a gorgeous, retired exotic dancer is fed up with her broke and boring lifestyle. The dreams promised by her husband, Bryce aren't coming true, and Seven's heart longs for the endless supply of cash she was forced to give up. When the bills aren't getting paid and they soon face eviction, Seven wants to return to her old ways, but Bryce refuses. However, unbeknownst to him, Seven has a scheme up her sleeve that involves prostitution even though she won't be the one turning tricks. Once the money starts to flow, vows are eventually broken, and unconditional love gets put to the test. This gritty tale of love vs. money will be sure to leave you speechless.

# IN STORES NOW...

# CHECK OUT THESE LCB SEQUELS

# STREET FICTION

"C.J. Hudson not only delivered a hot novel, but he also proved why he is called the `keyboard assassin'. Chedda Boyz is filled with sex, lies, murder, betrayal, deceit and revenge. It takes you on an action paced ride through Cleveland and leaves you with your mouth hanging open and wanting more."
*Amazon Review*

"Absolutely loved the book read it in 4 hours, great storyline and constant action. Not your typical urban fiction."
*Amazon Review*

**MAIL TO:**
PO Box 423
Brandywine, MD 20613
301-362-6508

**FAX TO:**
301-579-9913

# ORDER FORM

Ship to: _____

Address: _____

Date: _____ Phone: _____

Email: _____

City & State: _____ Zip: _____

*Make all money orders and cashiers checks payable to:* **Life Changing Books**

| Qty. | ISBN | Title | Release Date | Price |
|------|------|-------|--------------|-------|
| | 0-9741394-2-4 | Bruised by Azarel | Jul-05 | $ 15.00 |
| | 0-9741394-7-5 | Bruised 2: The Ultimate Revenge by Azarel | Oct-06 | $ 15.00 |
| | 0-9741394-3-2 | Secrets of a Housewife by J. Tremble | Feb-06 | $ 15.00 |
| | 0-9741394-6-7 | The Millionaire Mistress by Tiphani | Nov-06 | $ 15.00 |
| | 1-934230-99-5 | More Secrets More Lies by J. Tremble | Feb-07 | $ 15.00 |
| | 1-934230-95-2 | A Private Affair by Mike Warren | May-07 | $ 15.00 |
| | 1-934230-93-6 | Deep by Danette Majette | Jul-07 | $ 15.00 |
| | 1-934230-96-0 | Flexin & Sexin Volume 1 | Jun-07 | $ 15.00 |
| | 1-934230-89-8 | Still a Mistress by Tiphani | Nov-07 | $ 15.00 |
| | 1-934230-91-X | Daddy's House by Azarel | Nov-07 | $ 15.00 |
| | 1-934230-88-X | Naughty Little Angel by J. Tremble | Feb-08 | $ 15.00 |
| | 1-934230847 | In Those Jeans by Chantel Jolie | Jun-08 | $ 15.00 |
| | 1-934230820 | Rich Girls by Kendall Banks | Oct-08 | $ 15.00 |
| | 1-934230839 | Expensive Taste by Tiphani | Nov-08 | $ 15.00 |
| | 1-934230782 | Brooklyn Brothel by C. Stecko | Jan-09 | $ 15.00 |
| | 1-934230669 | Good Girl Gone bad by Danette Majette | Mar-09 | $ 15.00 |
| | 1-934230804 | From Hood to Hollywood by Sasha Raye | Mar-09 | $ 15.00 |
| | 1-934230707 | Sweet Swagger by Mike Warren | Jun-09 | $ 15.00 |
| | 1-934230677 | Carbon Copy by Azarel | Jul-09 | $ 15.00 |
| | 1-934230723 | Millionaire Mistress 3 by Tiphani | Nov-09 | $ 15.00 |
| | 1-934230715 | A Woman Scorned by Ericka Williams | Nov-09 | $ 15.00 |
| | 1-934230685 | My Man Her Son by J. Tremble | Feb-10 | $ 15.00 |
| | 1-924230731 | Love Heist by Jackie D. | Mar-10 | $ 15.00 |
| | 1-934230812 | Flexin & Sexin Volume 2 | Apr-10 | $ 15.00 |
| | 1-934230748 | The Dirty Divorce by Miss KP | May-10 | $ 15.00 |
| | 1-934230758 | Chedda Boyz by CJ Hudson | Jul-10 | $ 15.00 |
| | 1-934230766 | Snitch by VegasClarke | Oct-10 | $ 15.00 |
| | 1-934230693 | Money Maker by Tonya Ridley | Oct-10 | $ 15.00 |
| | 1-934230774 | The Dirty Divorce Part 2 by Miss KP | Nov-10 | $ 15.00 |
| | 1-934230170 | The Available Wife by Carla Pennington | Jan-11 | $ 15.00 |
| | 1-934230774 | One Night Stand by Kendall Banks | Feb-11 | $ 15.00 |
| | 1-934230278 | Bitter by Danette Majette | Feb-11 | $ 15.00 |
| | 1-934230299 | Married to a Balla by Jackie D. | May-11 | $ 15.00 |
| | 1-934230308 | The Dirty Divorce Part 3 by Miss KP | Jun-11 | $ 15.00 |
| | 1-934230316 | Next Door Nympho By CJ Hudson | Jun-11 | $ 15.00 |
| | 1-934230286 | Bedroom Gangsta by J. Tremble | Sep-11 | $ 15.00 |
| | 1-934230340 | Another One Night Stand by Kendall Banks | Oct-11 | $ 15.00 |
| | 1-934230359 | The Available Wife Part 2 by Carla Pennington | Nov-11 | $ 15.00 |
| | | | **Total for Books** | $ |
| | | | Shipping Charges (add $4.95 for 1-4 books*) | $ |
| | | | **Total Enclosed (add lines)** | $ |

\* **Prison Orders-** Please allow up to three (3) weeks for delivery.

Please Note: We are not held responsible for returned prison orders. Make sure the facility will receive books before ordering.

\*Shipping and Handling of 5-10 books is $6.95, please contact us if your order is more than 10 books. (301)362-6508